MATED TO THE VIKENS

INTERSTELLAR BRIDES® PROGRAM - BOOK 8

GRACE GOODWIN

GET A FREE BOOK!

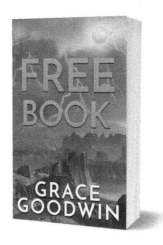

INTERSTELLAR BRIDES® PROGRAM

YOUR mate is out there. Take the test today and discover your perfect match. Are you ready for a sexy alien mate (or two)?

VOLUNTEER NOW!

interstellarbridesprogram.com

1

*S*ophia, *Interstellar Brides Processing Center, Earth*

HIS HANDS WERE SO SKILLED, STROKING OVER ME. I WAS ON a soft bed, the man beside me. I felt every hard inch of him press along my side as he learned me with the soft touch of his fingertips. They ran expertly over my bare flesh, making me shiver, making me gasp, making me eager for more. But his hand didn't stop.

My eyes were closed and I just reveled in the feel of him, and when I wanted more, he began to touch me with his other hand. One on my breast, the other sliding over the curls between my thighs.

"Open for me."

I didn't hesitate to comply with his husky order, parting my legs eagerly. Fingers slipped over my wet folds and taunted the eager bud.

The sound that escaped my lips was part moan, part

gasp. My arousal, which had been keen before, flared to life like a match on the driest of tinder. And when one digit slid deep inside me, I arched my back and cried out.

"Yes!"

"You like being filled, don't you?" he asked.

I nodded my head against the soft pillow.

"Do you want my cock?"

Did I? Did I want the single finger that curled and stroked deep inside me to be replaced by his cock?

"Yes," I breathed.

He took my hand in his and brought it down to his hard length. I wrapped my fingers around him, but my grip wouldn't close all the way. As I slid up and down the velvety length, I felt wetness seep onto my skin. The contact was hot, almost burning and I loosened my fingers.

"Do not be afraid." His hand came over mine as he began to stroke himself, showing me how he liked it, not allowing me to let go.

"My seed. You feel it, the power of it seeping into your skin?"

My palm was slick with his essence. It was so hot, almost burning, but it felt good. Too good. I was ready to come and he'd barely touched me.

"You're mine now. Your body knows it, recognizes my seed. Wants it. Needs it."

"Yes," I repeated. I could not deny him. While it seemed odd that I would react in such a visceral way to contact with his pre-cum, I wasn't going to question it. He was making me feel too good.

"She's ready for us." A second male voice spoke.

I turned my head, opened my eyes, but it was too dark

to make out anything more than silhouettes. Two men loomed over me, and when I felt another hand on my body, I knew both of them were touching me.

I wanted to move, to question why two men were in bed with me when the second man took my hand in his and directed it straight to his cock as well. Once I held him firmly, too, he let go and began touching me.

Two cocks! So big and thick, hot and hard. I felt the heat from the second man's pre-cum coat my fingers, seep into my skin. I gasped as my entire body heated, my blood becoming sluggish, my skin becoming slick with sweat.

"We'll both fuck you." The second man's voice was deeper, slower.

"What about me?" No, this wasn't the first man, or even the second. It was another man. A third!

Three? I struggled to breathe, completely overwhelmed. I couldn't release their cocks if I tried, the need to feel their pre-cum was too intense to resist. It was like a drug, making me feel frantic and desperate. I squirmed beneath their hands and cried out when the finger that was sliding in and out of my pussy, mimicking how I so desperately wanted to be fucked, pulled away.

I felt hands on my thighs pushing them wide, felt the wide crown of a cock sliding over my folds. It was the third man's, for I still stroked the others.

"Three of us, mate." The third man didn't delay, but slowly sank into me, stretching me open and filling me. Deeper and deeper he went until I felt his balls nudge against my bottom, felt his hips press into mine.

I groaned, never taking a cock such as his before. He remained still, embedded deep inside me.

"I need...please...move!" I cried.

"Our mate is a bossy little thing. Even being impaled on my cock, she gives orders."

The man was talking to the other two, not me.

"We will fuck you as you need," he replied.

"I *need* you to move."

A soft chuckle came from him. I could feel it in his body where it connected to mine.

"The seed power is intense from three men." It was the first man's voice. It was the only way I could tell them apart in the dark. I felt as if I were in a porno, for I had impossibly big cocks in my hands and another deep inside me. And I wanted it. Begged for it even.

The third man pulled his cock back, only the head inside me, before he plunged deep. I tilted my head back and cried out as he began to move.

"We won't last, mate. None of us will. We will give you our seed, ensure that you crave us. Need us. Need our cocks just as much as we need you."

I could do nothing but stroke the two cocks in my hands as the one fucking me had me pinned to the bed.

"I'm going to come." It was the second man's deep growl. I could feel him thicken in my palm just before I felt hot pulses of seed land on my belly and breasts.

Perhaps it was the knowledge that I'd stroked him off so well that he couldn't hold back. Perhaps it was the fact that I had a man fucking me as a second came all over me, but I came too. Hard. I screamed as I gave over to the pleasure of it all. I barely heard the first man's growl, but felt his seed coat my body. As the shimmering feel of the orgasm began to taper, their hands moved over my body, spreading their seed. It should have seemed weird, being coated in the sticky essence, but it heated my flesh wherever it touched. My nipples hardened and I clenched down on the cock that fucked me with wild abandon.

"She's so tight I can't hold off."

His body stiffened above me as he shouted out, his seed pumping into me. I'd never imagined I could feel a man's release inside me, but his was hot and copious, coating my walls, sliding out around his thick cock. I came again, the need too great.

"Such a good girl. You are ours. You belong to all of us. Our seed is on you. In you. We have not formally claimed you, but we will when you are ready. There is no going back. You will desire us always, as we do you."

"Yes. Again. More, please." I'd forgotten I still held their cocks, both remaining as thick and hard as if they hadn't just come. They shifted, their cocks slipping from my fingers.

The man between my legs pulled out.

"More," I begged.

I sensed them shifting on the bed, moving so that a different man was between my thighs. I was flipped onto my belly, a hand about my waist pulling me back for the next man's cock.

"Yes, more," the deep voice said. "Always."

I whimpered as he filled me, collapsing as my body convulsed in another orgasm, my pussy rippling over his cock.

"Miss Antonelli!"

A woman's voice. Confused, I hung on to pleasure as the aftershocks of the orgasm made me shake and moan.

And that huge cock fucked me, filled me, stretched me with relentless force.

God, I wanted more, but the sensations faded no matter how I clung to them.

"Miss Antonelli, are you all right?"

My eyes fluttered open and saw a familiar face looming over me. It wasn't one of the men who'd been in bed with me. It was a woman, one I recognized all too well. Her face was pretty, but severe, as if she took her job very seriously. Warden Egara. The woman who worked for *them*. The alien races who claimed to be protecting our planet from some terrible horde of creatures. "Warden Egara?"

"You screamed. Are you hurt?"

"I...you heard me scream?" God, I'd come so hard that I'd screamed? Who else heard me lose it?

She nodded, but remained silent.

"Sorry." I looked around and wondered exactly how thin the walls were in this place. The room looked like a medical office, the walls white and the furniture clinical, unwelcoming.

Of course, no one stayed long. The brides and soldiers were processed in different sections of the building. So, there might be a whole squadron of soldiers on the other side of the wall listening to me have an orgasm all over some alien cock. Who heard me scream? Probably everyone in the building. The tingling after-effects of the orgasm still pulsed in my body. My core clenched, eager for the man's hard cock to fill me once more. My nipples were hard and my skin was soaked in sweat.

I was supposed to be matched to the perfect alien

mate with some high-tech program. But that hadn't exactly been a test. No, that was more like being tossed into a live-stream adult film.

"Was that the test, the matching protocol I read about?"

Warden Egara raised both brows, a slight grin lifting the right side of her mouth. "Yes."

"What kind of test was that?" I asked.

She looked over me critically, as if still worried about my health. But my question appeared to ease her worry and the intense crease between her brows relaxed. "Intense, isn't it?"

That wasn't the only word I'd use. Incredible. Exhilarating. Overwhelming.

I nodded as I licked my lips. My hands were restrained in the testing chair and I wore the ugliest hospital gown ever to grace the female form. Dark gray with little Interstellar Brides Program insignia all over it, I felt like I was in a psych ward, not an alien dating service.

My nose chose that moment to itch and I sighed, resigning myself to twitching my face to relieve the sensation. I wasn't surprised by the thick restraints on my wrists and ankles. In fact, I'd grown quite used to them, for I'd been in handcuffs enough over the past few months.

Leaning back in the curved chair, I stared at the ceiling and tried to get my bearings. That dream, God, it had to have been a dream, had been the most amazing thing ever. It was the best dream I'd had since I'd been arrested. In fact, it had been the only dream. Nightmares, on the other hand, haunted me every time I dared close my eyes and try to rest.

7

"Is the testing over?" I asked. If she needed to do that again, I wouldn't object.

I rolled my head to the side to watch as she ran her fingers over the small tablet she held. "Yes, the testing is finished."

"So I've been matched?"

She looked up, offered me a quick smile, then glanced at the tablet again. "Yes. To Viken."

Viken. I'd heard of the small planet that was part of the Interstellar Coalition, but that was all. Earth hadn't been involved for long and I'd been too busy with legal proceedings and survival to waste time reading about alien civilizations.

She walked to a small desk against the wall on the opposite side of the testing room and sat down. "I need to ask some additional questions to continue your processing. For the record, please state your name."

"Sophia Antonelli."

"And the crime for which you were convicted?"

"Fraud. Money Laundering. Forgery. Illegal transport of goods across state lines. Smuggling." There were a couple more, smaller offenses, but that about covered the laundry list. "Is that sufficient?"

"Yes, that will do." Warden Egara's fingers flew across her tablet as she continued. "Are you currently, or have you ever been married?"

"No." I'd been married to my job, not a man. I'd been an art dealer, nothing exotic. Hell, what could be so harmless about a degree in Art History? Look where that got me. In prison, where the only chance to avoid long, miserable years of confinement meant volunteering to be an alien's bride.

"Have you produced biological offspring?"

"No." You had to have sex to get pregnant, and I was living a two-year dry spell.

"For the record, Miss Antonelli, as an eligible, fertile female in your prime, you had two options available to you to serve out your sentence, twenty-five years in the Carswell Penitentiary located in Fort Worth, Texas."

"No, thank you." Prison orange was not my color.

Warden Egara smiled patiently and continued on in a monotone voice, as if reading the words. "Or volunteer service in the Interstellar Brides Program. I am pleased to tell you that the system has made a successful match and you will be sent to a member planet. As a bride, you might never return to Earth, as all travel will be determined and controlled by your new planet's laws and customs. You will surrender your citizenship of Earth and become an official citizen of your new world."

I hadn't really thought about that. How could I not be a citizen of Earth? Was that even possible?

My belly clenched as the full impact of my decision settled in my bones. There was a small amount of time each day, seconds really, when I had yet to fully awaken, that I forgot what I'd become. Forgot what the Corellis had done to me and just how far I'd fallen.

"Your convictions carry a twenty-five-year sentence, yet you've elected to serve out your sentence under the direction of the Interstellar Brides Program. You have been assigned to a mate per testing protocols and will be transported off-planet, never to return to Earth. Do you understand what this alternative entails?"

"Yes." I wouldn't survive a year in prison, let alone two decades. I'd been incarcerated for six months awaiting trial, and that had felt like six years. Any alternative was better than a prison cell. One man. Three. Whatever. The true price was a one-way ticket to outer space. I was going to be just like the brides I'd read about in history books, the mail-order brides sent to the Wild West. I was going on a grand adventure and hoping for the best.

Not that I had a choice. I had no reason to stay on Earth. The Corelli family had ruined my life's work and my reputation. My business assets had been seized. I had no job, no contacts, no life. And, the bottom line? I *had* committed the crimes. Yes, the Corellis had threatened me, bullied me, but I'd still had a choice.

As much as I wished I'd never made the bargain with Vincent Corelli for the money to pay for my mother's expensive cancer treatments, I wouldn't trade the extra time with her for anything.

I'd do it all again. So what if I'd smuggled his merchandise inside my art shipments in trade? I never hurt anyone. And when my mother finally did die, I'd assumed my work with the mafia was finished.

That had not been the case. Vincent Corelli wasn't eager to give up a reliable mule. He'd threatened to kill me then, and I hadn't pushed the issue. That was until I'd been caught with a crate full of blood diamonds and assault rifles and hauled off to jail.

Vincent Corelli didn't bail me out, and I didn't talk to the feds. I didn't tell anyone he'd been blackmailing me. I still had family on the outside. My cousin's two kids weren't even five years old. And yeah, I'd grown up in New York. I knew how things worked.

I kept my mouth shut, my extended family went on about their lives, and Corelli let me take the fall.

So I had nothing left. No one. My world was destroyed. So I'd make a new one. On Viken.

Fiddling with the tablet some more, she frowned. "Your match is not as strong as I would like."

"It's not strong? What does that mean?" I asked, shifting in the hard seat. I felt like I was at the dentist with my naked backside stuck to the damn chair.

"Our matches are typically over ninety-nine percent. Yours is only eight-five."

I frowned, too. "Does that mean I can't go?" Prison? Really? And I'd just psyched myself up for this whole alien bride deal.

She did some more finger swiping, then stilled. "Interesting."

I began to shake, a thousand butterflies dancing in my stomach. I was *not* getting back onto the prison bus, shackled and forced into a horrible orange jumpsuit. I couldn't do it.

She looked at me again, offered a brilliant smile. "It seems that you have been matched to three Viken warriors."

I swallowed, thought about the dream. Three men. Three sets of hands. Three cocks.

"Three?" Holy crap. Three? What the hell was I supposed to do with three men?

She nodded. "Your match is lower than usual because you have three mates. I think eighty-five percent is quite remarkable for three." She cocked her head to the side as she studied me. "You do not seem surprised. I assumed you would be shocked."

"The dream," I replied. I didn't say more, for I was not

going to recount how I was fucked by one man while I stroked two others off.

"There were three men in your simulation? Interesting. The last Earth woman matched to Viken was matched to three men as well, however they are triplets and genetically identical. Perhaps you experienced their mating ritual."

"Are you telling me that was real?" Holy shit. I wanted to experience that for real. If I was going to have three men touching me like that, I didn't mind going to Viken at all. In fact, I was ready.

"Yes. The experience *was* real, but someone else's recorded neural experience. A different couple. Or...um, foursome. Out of all the simulations that flitted across your brain as part of the testing, this one was your match."

My nipples hardened in agreement at the memory. Yes, that was definitely a match.

"There is a note here." Her brow furrowed as she read. Finished, she lifted her gaze to me. "This makes sense now. It appears Viken has instituted a brand new mating protocol for the Interstellar Brides Program. Since their Queen came through the program, and her match to the triplets was so successful in uniting their planet, it has been decreed that other Viken males from the three different sectors now share a mate as well." She waved her hand in the air. "I'm sure they will explain everything once you arrive."

"That's it?" I asked as she stood. "I just... go?"

"You're right. There is one last question. Do you accept the results of the testing?"

"I do."

"Sophia Antonelli, you are no longer a citizen of Earth, but of Viken. Good luck."

The wall opened behind me and I saw a soft pale blue glow. My seat moved, as if on wheels. She patted my shoulder as I passed through the wall and was lowered into a vat of warm water. I felt instantly soothed, surrounded by protection, comfort.

I didn't even mind the giant needle-like thing headed for the side of my skull.

Frowning, I turned from the strange, robotic arm to look back at the warden.

"Don't worry, dear. That just implants your NPU so you can speak their language."

Blinking, confused, I winced at the small pinch of pain behind my ear.

Damn. That was going to leave a mark.

Warden Egara smiled and stepped back as the wall began to move. Soon, I would be locked in this little room, in this blue water. Were they going to drown me?

Frantic now, I yanked on the restraints as the warden continued to smile.

"Your transport will begin in three...two...one."

The blue water came to my chin and everything went black.

2

*E*rik, *Planet Viken, Viken United Compound, Transport Center*

Nerves made my heart beat faster than I wished as I watched my two brothers-in-arms. Gunnar, with his black hair and blacker heart, stood silent and still as a statue as we waited for our mate to arrive via transport. He'd vowed not to love her, but Rolf and I didn't need him to do so.

"How long must we wait?" Gunnar turned on the Viken warrior behind the transport station, every line in his body screaming of his irritation.

"For someone not interested in a mate, you're fucking impatient," I countered. While the other two stood near the transport area, I leaned against the wall.

Gunnar regarded me over his shoulder with a look that screamed *fuck you*.

"Not long, sir," the attendant said. "The transport

signal is strong. Your mate should arrive in the next few minutes."

"Relax, Gunnar," Rolf said. He could always calm our friend. "Earth is a long way from here. A long, long way."

They stood shoulder to shoulder. Next to Gunnar's darkness, Rolf looked like a beacon. Always smiling, his pale blond hair and bright green eyes nearly made him glow in the transport room's artificial light. His easy smile and natural charm had served us well over the years. Women took one look at Gunnar and either ran away or lay down at his feet like slaves awaiting orders from a master. But Rolf? They hung on his every word, offered him everything. They fell in love with him as easily as rain fell from the sky. One was light, the other dark.

Females fell at their feet, but neither warrior loved in return. I'd fought by their sides for a decade in the Hive war. We had bled and killed together. I knew these men better than I knew myself, and they did not love.

Neither did I. We were all broken. But when the Queen you've sworn to protect, the leaders you've laid down your life to keep safe, ask you to take a mate, to help them unite the three sectors, refusal is not an option.

"Did you two see her profile?" I asked. Less than an hour ago, our mate's information had been transmitted to us from Earth. Sophia. We knew her name and that she was some sort of smuggler, convicted of crimes on her home world. But that mattered not, for we were not perfect men. We'd killed, and worse, during the wars, and learned to live with it. Sophia promised us a new beginning, a new chapter in our dark lives. The report stated she was twenty-six years of age, young but ripe. I had stared at her image, looked into eyes nearly as dark as Gunnar's, and my cock had grown hard. It was impossible not to want her as we looked at her Earthen beauty. I'd been stunned to discover an alien female that stirred my cock.

"No need." Gunnar crossed his arms over his chest.

Years ago, when we'd first met, he'd been dressed head to toe in the black, as were all warriors from Sector Two. The sector uniform had been replaced by the space camouflage of the Coalition Fleet. Years later, we now served and wore the uniform for Viken United, the one bastion of peace on the planet, and our capital city. While we served the same command, he wore the black once more, as I wore brown and Rolf dark green. Each uniform's color represented the sector in which we were born. But on each of our arms a bright red band made us brothers. Red for Viken United, for our future queen, the beautiful baby Allayna.

Rolf laughed. "No need? What is wrong with you, Gunnar? Were you not curious?"

I shook my head as I pushed off the wall to move beside the attendant, to watch over his shoulder at the controls. I already knew exactly what Gunnar would say.

"No," he replied. "She is our mate. Her appearance is irrelevant."

Rolf smacked him on the shoulder as he rolled his eyes. "Right. So if she's covered in warts and hideous to behold, you'll close your eyes and rut into her tight little pussy anyway?"

Gunnar raised his brow, clearly not amused. "She comes from Earth. The planet of Queen Leah, who is lovely. She was also matched to all three of us using the Bride matching program. I have no doubt I will find her adequate to our needs. She has to be. That's what the fucking testing was for."

Adequate to our needs. Right. We needed to fuck her, get her pregnant, and fulfill the Queen's decree. That was hard enough, but we also had to make our mate happy. With Gunnar a cranky bastard and the three of us not too keen on becoming emotionally involved, that would be the much more difficult task.

Clearly annoyed, Rolf turned to me. "I assume you could not resist temptation, Erik, and read her profile. I was on patrol and could not learn about her. Tell me everything." He bumped into Gunnar with his shoulder. If anyone else treated him with such casual disrespect, Gunnar would have ripped him to pieces by now. "And tell Gunnar, too. He's only pretending not to care."

Gunnar scowled but did not refute Rolf's claim. I stared at the empty transport pad and thought of our mate. "Her name is Sophia. Her hair is long and golden, like the bark of a Nerbu tree. Her eyes are dark brown, nearly as dark as Gunnar's."

I stopped speaking then as my cock hardened in my pants. Her body was small but well curved, her breasts just large enough to fill both my hands. Her small, tight ass begged to be spanked a bright pink. Her lips were full and a deep rose color I hungered to taste.

"Erik?" Rolf leaned forward, amusement on his face, waiting.

"What?"

"Golden hair and dark eyes. What else?" He circled his hand to get me to continue.

I shook my head and adjusted my cock in my pants.

"You were too lazy to look for yourself, you'll just have to wait."

"Transport imminent," the attendant said.

Gunnar shrugged and turned to stare at the platform. We all did as the familiar humming vibration started. The buzzing sensation traveled up through my boots and into my legs as the transport pad powered up, ready to receive our new bride.

"I hope this isn't a huge fucking mistake." Rolf's worry was one I shared. But the Bride Program's testing was practically infallible. It matched not only to obvious likes and dislikes, but subconscious ones as well. And considering she'd also been matched to Gunnar, I eagerly awaited our first chance to fuck her. Gunnar belonged to an exclusive order of warriors who needed to dominate their lovers. If Sofia had been matched to us, then I couldn't wait to discover her reaction to my firm hand on her bare bottom or my cock filling her from behind as Gunnar or Rolf claimed her wet pussy.

"If this is a mistake, we will endure and honor our Queen's wishes." Gunnar's grumbling response was typical. *Do what needed to be done*. That was Gunnar. His philosophy made him merciless in battle, and in bed. We'd shared women before, many times, but it was always Gunnar whose quiet and ruthless temperament broke them open, who made them writhe and beg and scream for release. I had neither the patience nor the desire to own any woman's soul. Gunnar had a collection, a pool of pets eager to answer any time he called. He loved none of them, had sworn to turn them all away once we claimed a mate. And he would. He might be a surly bastard, but there was no one more honorable.

I sincerely hoped our Sophia would be able to handle what Gunnar would demand of her. She would. The matching would see to it.

Me? I wanted to fuck a beautiful female, to fill her with my seed and mark her as my own. Having both Gunnar and Rolf to help me protect what was mine—ours—made our forced match easier to accept.

No matter what happened, she would be safe. Protected. Civil war brewed on Viken, and I would not take a mate knowing she might be left unprotected like my mother had been. My mother's fate would not befall another.

"Receiving transport." The technician's voice held excitement, anticipation. The arrival of an Interstellar Bride was always celebrated on Viken, for it happened rarely, and only once before from Earth. That had been the Queen. Most of our warriors mated before they came home from the war with the Hive, or chose a bride from their home sector.

I stepped forward as her outline took shape on the transport pad. Luscious curves wrapped in a dark red dress. As the transport light faded, Gunnar stepped forward to inspect our bride, but I lifted my hand to stop him. He stilled feet from her.

"Don't. Something is wrong." The woman's back was to us, but her hair was a dark auburn instead of nearly black. And before her, I saw movement, as if she were not alone.

———

SOPHIA

．　．　．

I EXPECTED BEING TRANSPORTED TO BE SOMETHING LIKE watching an old *Star Trek* TV show, where Spock disappeared in one place and reappeared in another. For me, it was like being put under for a surgery and waking up somewhere new with no memory of how I had arrived. The last thing I remembered was the warden counting backwards. Now, I was being dragged across a cold floor. My brain too sluggish to react, I did not resist.

"What the fuck are we going to do? She's not the fucking Queen. Where's the damn baby?" one man shouted from just above my head as he dragged me by my arms. Seconds later, the cruel grip of the unknown man released me and I slumped back onto the floor, my head striking just hard enough to make me wish I were still unconscious. The air was cool, but not cold. Humid. It smelled like churned earth, as if a garden had been tilled. It was an unexpected scent, but it was obvious I wasn't in the antiseptic testing center in Miami any longer.

The panicked tone of the man's voice had me thinking something went wrong. I opened my eyes, blinking them a few times, trying to regain my wits after what felt like a really long nap.

"Obviously, something went wrong during transport." There was a second man. His voice was calmer, deeper, and came from the direction of my feet.

Something went wrong? Obviously, if I was being dragged about, unconscious. Or, they at least thought me that way.

I assumed I was in the transport center on Viken, but

it was not as I expected. No *Star Trek* space deck. The walls were painted dark gray, the ceiling low. There was a window on the far wall and beyond the glass all I could see was green. All green, as if I were in the middle of a forest. Directly in front of me was a tall platform with strange symbols and buttons, screens with data flowing across them that I could not read. The language was odd and unfamiliar. I had to assume it was the alien control station for transport. Just beyond it was a raised platform, the shiny surface empty. Was that where I'd arrived? Had they dragged me off that platform and dropped me like garbage on the floor?

I could see their legs. Both wore dark pants and black boots. I was afraid to move to see more of them, for their focus was not on me and I had no wish to draw their attention. After dealing with the Corellis, I knew it was sometimes best to be completely invisible. Surely, these two brutes were not my mates. If so, where was the third?

"Where is the Queen, Ensign? Where the fuck is the princess?" the second man asked.

"I don't know, sir."

"What do you mean, you don't know? What the fuck am I supposed to tell Vikter?"

"There was no indication of a malfunction." The panicked man with the low rank appeared to be the poor guy who worked here, wherever here was. The other, the angry one, I had no idea about.

"Then who the hell is this female?"

There had been some kind of problem with transport. It sounded as if they'd been expecting someone else. Where in the world was I? No. Where in the universe was I? Had I really been transported to Viken?

"I don't know, sir. Are you sure it's not the Queen? She's clearly human. Look at her skin. No Viken female has skin that soft."

"Is her hair red as flame?"

"No."

"It's not the fucking Queen, you fool."

"I don't know what went wrong. As you saw, she just... just appeared."

"Yes, but from where?" I heard the anger. The men moved a few steps toward me and I saw an arm point in my direction. Long sleeve, black shirt, a man's hand. The rest of him was hidden behind the table. "Find out who she is. She's not Queen Leah, but perhaps Vikter will have a use for her."

No, I wasn't a queen. The men were obviously up to no good. And they'd called me human. Mentioned Viken. Clearly, I was no longer on Earth. Which was bad. But at least I knew where I was, and it wasn't some crazy planet I'd never heard of.

"Yes, sir."

It was obvious who was in charge of the duo. "Whoever was expecting her will trace her transport to these coordinates. I can't be here when they arrive."

"What? I can't be here either!" The ensign's voice went up an octave, his words hurried and clipped, panicked.

"This was *your* mistake. That female, and whoever comes looking for her, is *your* problem."

The guy in charge pointed again, this time the cuff of his shirt rode up and I saw a tattoo on the inside of his wrist. It looked like a three-headed snake.

"Transport me to the Central City transport station as planned. No one will track me among that crowd."

"But what am I to do with her?" The ensign came around the control station and I closed my eyes, pretended to be asleep.

His footsteps were close and I felt a vibration in the floor. A deep hum filled the air around me, made the hair on my body stand at attention.

"Transport me and find out who she is. If she's not royalty or worth a ransom, kill her."

Kill her?

"What if she's worth something?"

"Keep her alive. You know who to contact."

My eyes popped open at that and I stared at the ensign's legs as a bright yellow light filled the room then went out. The vibrations stopped and the noise cut off abruptly.

The ensign was breathing hard and whispering to himself, mumbling about unification, and a baby, and assholes.

Oh shit. Was he going to kill me? Seriously?

Hysterical laughter bubbled up in my gut but I held it back by sheer force of will. I'd left Earth to get away from corrupt assholes just like this one and the one who'd transported away. Instead, it was like I'd never left at all. This was exactly how the mafia operated back home. The Corellis controlled everything that went on in New York, including me.

Stupid to believe I'd be free of unethical men and organized crime. People were people everywhere in the universe, it seemed, and even the exalted Coalition of Planets hadn't managed to get rid of criminals like these two and whomever they worked for. I'd been transported across the universe and landed right back where I started, mixed up in something. Something bad. And I was going to pay the price. Again.

He frowned and I had to tilt my chin back slightly to watch as he paced. For a killer, he seemed really nervous about it. That played in my favor. I wouldn't remain on the floor just waiting for him to kill me.

I looked down, shocked to see that I now wore a dress. Was this part of the bride processing? The gown was long sleeved and the hem, when I stood, would fall to my ankles. The cut was simple but flattering, fitting snugly to my small breasts and flared at the hips to emphasize a woman's body. The color was a plain blue, but the fabric was soft as silk and clung to every curve.

Not exactly commando gear.

I wiggled my toes inside soft, leather slippers and wished I had steel-toed boots to kick this guy in the balls.

Lying like the dead, I watched him from beneath my lashes as he paced, looked at me, looked away. He laughed maniacally as he ran his fingers through his dark hair. If he was a typical Viken man, then they looked pretty much like men on Earth. He was a little bigger than the men I knew, but I didn't know if that was a Viken thing or if he was just big.

"Stupid fucking transport codes. Not the fucking queen," he mumbled to himself.

With the vibrations, the bright yellow light and other man gone, I was positive I was in some sort of transport center, although the room looked old and long forgotten, paint peeling and malfunctioning lights at odd intervals along the gray walls. The room was tiny. The transport pad looked big enough to hold three or four people and the only door in or out was to my left.

I waited for the ensign to turn away from me. I leapt to my feet, making a run for it, hoping I had surprise on my side.

I gripped the door's handle and pushed. Relief flooded me as the door opened and I raced outside. My dress tangled around my ankles and I stumbled, taking two short steps before the guy grabbed me from behind.

"Get back here!" he snarled, spinning me around.

I faced him, feeling like a toddler as he towered over me. His grip on my arm tightened and he cursed.

"Gods be damned, you're so fucking small. I don't want to do this."

Small? Sure, I was five-two without heels, but I wasn't going to debate with him if he didn't want to kill me.

"Then don't. Just let me go. I won't say anything. I promise." My heart was in my throat.

His dark eyes were frantic and I could tell he wasn't a cold-blooded killer. I'd met enough of Corelli's enforcers to recognize fear when I saw it. He was more like one of the Corelli family's new recruits, young and wet behind the ears. But often, those were the most dangerous because they'd been backed into a corner with no way out.

He shook his head, debating what to do. "I'd be a dead man if they found out."

"No one will ever know. I swear."

He studied me, his grip painful. "Who are you? Who's coming for you?"

"No one." At least, no one I knew. Warden Egara had promised me that I was being sent to three Viken mates, but I had no idea if they would even know anything had happened to me.

"You were transporting to Viken United. Why?"

"I don't know."

His eyes narrowed. "You're a bride. A fucking Interstellar Bride."

My eyes widened when he spat the truth and I shook my head, trying to think of a lie, anything to get him to let me go.

"Don't bother with your lies." He reached behind him with his free hand and pulled out a gun. Yes, it was a gun. A space gun, but I'd seen enough to know. It was shiny metal, bright like silver. It was small, too small, but that didn't mean it wasn't powerful. I didn't see a place for bullets, but dead was dead, bullet or not. "You're a bride. Gods be damned. Who's coming for you?"

"I don't know," I repeated, my voice rising in my panic.

He snarled at me. "Fuck. Your mate will probably bring an entire fucking squadron to hunt me down."

I shook my head. "No. I've never even met him." I wasn't going to tell him I had three mates.

"Shut up." Sweat dripped from his brow to his cheek and the veins at his temples bulged just under his skin. He was afraid, and that wasn't good for my odds of survival. "It doesn't fucking matter. Don't you get it? He'll come for you. A fucking warrior's bride."

I tugged on my arm, trying to break free. "Let me go!" I shouted.

"He'll come for you, all right. And fucking rip me in half." His grip tightened until I cried out in pain, worried he'd break one of the bones in my arm, or dislocate a shoulder. "Fucking bride. How did this happen? I'm doomed. Fucking doomed!"

Rage fueled my courage. I'd let the Corellis scare me into cooperating, doing anything and everything they wanted. Even after my mother was dead and buried, they forced me to smuggle for them. Drugs. Money. Technology. Art. Diamonds. They threatened to kill me, and I'd done what they wanted. I'd cowed down and let them rule me. And for what? All I got out of it was a prison sentence and a one-way ticket to this ass-backward planet. Fuck this.

I pulled back and kneed him in the groin with every ounce of strength I had. "Asshole!"

He dropped like a stone, but wouldn't release his grip, nearly dragging me to the ground with him. The gun was in his free hand and he aimed it at my face where it hovered mere inches above his own. I grabbed his wrist with both hands and shoved, hard, forcing the point of the weapon away from me. It fired once, the sound like a bottle rocket exploding between us. A white blast of light shot out and pulsed toward the trees.

Growling, he rolled onto his side and tried to push me to the ground, but I held on to his wrist with all my might. I was breathing hard and my feet were tangled in the dress. With my arms busy, I used my legs again, kneed him once more. Either Viken men had bionic balls or his adrenaline was running as high as mine. All the strike did was make him suck in his breath and allow me to come down on top of him where he lay flat on his back. I loomed over him, looked into his dark, angry eyes, but he still had the gun.

"I'm going to kill you," he growled.

"Go ahead and try, you asshole." Something inside me snapped, and with it went all my fear. If I died here, so be it, but I was tired of being afraid. Bullied. Used by powerful men who treated me like an expendable pawn. I bent down, sinking my teeth deep into the flesh of his hand until I felt my teeth break through flesh to meat and my mouth flooded with blood.

He howled in pain and pulled his arm away from me, toward his chest and I pushed my advantage. I had no idea where my strength came from, perhaps my rage at the Corellis poured out of me, but I was able to bend his wrist at an odd angle and push down. His arm collapsed at the odd angle and I fell on top of him. The hand he'd used to hold the gun lay trapped between us. I arched my back, trying to keep my body out of his line of fire as I twisted his wrist even more, hoping to hear bone snap.

I heard a pop, saw a slight flare of bright light. Not his wrist. The weapon had been fired.

Had I been shot? For a split second, I panicked, worried my rage and shock would block the pain of my injury. I gritted my teeth and tried to focus on my body, but I felt nothing but the racing beat of my heart as I fought to draw air in and out of my body. I shook, each shuddering breath a struggle as I blinked slowly, trying to understand. Everything felt like it was happening in slow motion and I watched with a detachment I could hardly fathom.

His legs became lax as the fight left him. Beneath me, his body softened as his muscles relaxed. His hold on my arm loosened and his hand slid to the ground. He looked at me with wide eyes, as if stunned. Pushing away from his chest, I grabbed the gun and scrambled backward on my hands and knees, away from him.

The light shining through the uppermost canopy of

trees filtered down to dance on his chest, the blood coating the front of his shirt spread in a bright red bloom over the dark green fabric.

So, the Vikens bled red, just like humans.

I watched him fade, the taste of his blood in my mouth twisted my stomach and I rolled to my side as my body was racked with dry heaves. I hadn't eaten in long hours, and for once, I was thankful for an empty stomach.

Chilled to the bone, I turned away from him and climbed to my feet. I stood on shaky legs and saw that his eyes had become glassy and blank. My heart thundered in my ears but the rest of me felt completely numb.

He was dead. I killed him.

I jerked my head around, left then right, looking for more enemies, more threats. We were in the center of a clearing with only the small building, squat and covered in what appeared to be moss. I turned, slowly, and felt like I'd stepped into a magical forest. Tall trees loomed like skyscrapers overhead, so thick and green I could barely see the color of the sky beyond. The ground was soft beneath my feet, springy with a mixture of moss and thick, lush grass.

I felt as if I'd walked into a Monet painting. I longed to have my paints so I could put the incredible beauty to canvas. It was... perfection. Everything was damp, as if it had just rained. Verdant and humid, sweat gathered on my brow as the sounds of animals I didn't know chirped and squawked from their hidden roosts. Climbing vines wound their way from tree to tree, and every few inches along their length an exotic flower, larger than my open palm, decorated the forest with vibrant pink and purple, orange and gold petals. Viken was lovely. Colorful. Strangely beautiful and I wanted to paint it all.

Except for the dead man at my feet.

I looked down at the strange weapon in my hand, pointed it at the ground a few feet away and squeezed. Nothing happened. I tried again and again, but the weapon was useless.

Irritated, I tossed the gun aside and turned my back on the small building. I needed water, something to get the taste of death out of my mouth, but I couldn't go back into the transport center. What if the man with the tattoo came back to finish what the ensign had started? What if someone else did?

I had to get away. I wasn't safe here, even with this man now dead. Even with nature all around me. I had no idea where I was. There could be others about who would find me. How would I explain the dead body?

Walking into the woods, I didn't look back. I was an alien here. They'd see the dead Viken and I'd be looking at a murder charge. Why would anyone listen to me? I was from Earth. I was on another planet. Were there any laws governing the right to kill in self-defense on Viken? God, I couldn't go to prison. That was why I volunteered for the Brides Program in the first place.

First things first, I had to put as much distance as possible between myself and this fucking horror story.

The woods closed around me and I kept walking until the small building disappeared from my view. Looking around, I saw no obvious path and had no idea which way to go. The forest looked the same in every direction.

It didn't matter which way I chose, as long as I ran far, far away.

I picked up the hem of my dress and dashed through leaves and vines, wound my way past trees and flowers, and kept moving until my legs ached and my lungs burned.

I'd survived on Earth with the Corellis. I would keep going until I found some people who looked friendly enough to ask for help. The language thing that giant needle had poked into my skull as part of my processing on Earth must have worked, because I'd understood the two men who'd wanted me dead all too well.

Yes, running was a risk. But staying, waiting for tattoo man to come back and finish the job, seemed worse.

I found a small stream and rinsed my mouth, splashed water on my face and kept moving.

Yeah, I might die out here. But at this point, I had nothing left to lose.

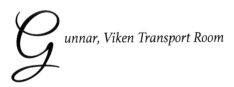

unnar, Viken Transport Room

THE TECHNICIAN HAD A BETTER ANGLE THAN I, AND HE paled, swaying on his feet. "My Queen?"

She sat slowly, a baby in her lap, both with dark red hair. The Queen turned to face me, confusion written on her face. "Where am I? Gunnar? Erik? What is going on?"

"Wolf!" Baby Allayna lifted her arms when she saw one of her favorite playmates, Rolf. The tiny girl could not say his name properly, and so he'd become Wolf. I learned from the Queen that a wolf was an animal on Earth, fierce and loyal, ruthless and cunning. She considered it to be apt, for my friend was all those things.

Rolf hurried forward and lifted Allayna from Queen Leah's arms.

I bowed my head and stepped forward, offering my

hand to assist her from the transport pad. "My Queen, what are you doing here?"

She looked around, confused. "We were transporting to Sector Three. My mates are already there, awaiting our arrival."

Erik barked at the transport technician. "Contact the transport room in Sector Three immediately. Her mates will be ready to tear the place apart."

"Yes, sir." The wide-eyed technician followed Erik's order, his voice clipped but firm as he contacted the other transport room and let Queen Leah's mates, Tor, Lev and Drogan, know that their mate and daughter were both alive and well.

"Transport imminent. Please clear the pad," the technician yelled the warning, and I tugged on the Queen's hand until she was safely behind me as the transport pad fired up once more.

Seconds later, Lev stood on the platform, his scowl made fierce by the scar running through his brow above his right eye. Lev was one of our triplet kings, but he'd been raised in Sector Two, my sector. He was the most ruthless of the brothers, the most feared. There was no forgiveness in him, no softness, at least not until Queen Leah.

Leah cried out and ran into his arms. "Lev!"

We silently watched him transform from tense warrior to comforting mate as he held her close. He lifted his arm in a silent command for Rolf to bring his daughter to him. Rolf stepped forward and Lev lifted the tiny girl into his arms as if she were the most delicate glass. A shudder racked the King's body. The little one nuzzled into her father's neck and I had to turn away. I could not stand the sight of so powerful a warrior broken by fear for his loved ones.

He was decimated by just a transport malfunction. Witnessing such vulnerability served as an effective yet simple reminder that it was better not to love. To risk such complete despair over a mate.

With his mate and daughter safely in his arms, Lev's attention turned to me. His jaw was tense, his eyes fierce. "What the fuck is going on here, Gunnar?"

I slowly shook my head, not cowed by the King's harsh tone. "We don't know, sir. We gathered to await the arrival of our mate from Earth."

Lev looked around, his arm tightening about his lovely mate's waist. I doubted he would let her go anytime soon. Leah clung to him with complete trust. But even Lev, a ruler of our planet, had not been able to keep his mate safe in something as simple as a transport. She could have been sent anywhere.

"VSS?" Lev looked to the transport technician when he spoke. "And did you confirm transport from Earth?"

"Yes, sir."

"Then where is their mate?" The King's tone was clipped, but the younger man shrugged.

"I don't know, sir. We'll have to run detailed analysis of the system signals. This type of mid-transport coordinate shift is impossible."

"Erik. Find out what the fuck is going on." I ordered my friend to take over transport control without a second thought. Erik had a special gift for technology, for puzzles. If we faced an enemy, I preferred a head-to-head confrontation. Rolf, the trickster, always talking, would try to manipulate or confuse his enemy before a strike. But Erik excelled at solving unsolvable puzzles, and for understanding our technology in a way I never could. His ability to rebuild communication pods and weapons had saved all our lives on more than one mission on the front line of the Interstellar Coalition's war with the Hive.

Erik frowned, his long dark hair pulled back and tied behind his head like a shadow. His fingers raced over the control panels as he ran an analysis with the much younger, less-experienced transport technician watching with dawning awe. "I don't know, Gunnar. It looks like the transport beams crossed and both of the women were redirected."

"Was Sophia sent to Sector Three in the Queen's place?" Rolf asked, his tone tense. He was always so calm, but now, he had the dark, commanding look usually reserved for Erik or myself. His fair coloring and easy manner fooled so many, hiding the pain he carried inside.

I paced as Erik made contact with Sector Three's transport, eager to know our mate was safe.

Our mate. *Sophia.* I'd lied to my brothers-in-arms when telling them I had not studied her profile. I had, in fact, memorized every detail. I knew the exact curve of her cheek, the golden flecks of color that made her right eye slightly lighter than her left. I'd read her entire application data log. Knew she was too small, too fragile, too fucking pure for a man like me. But none of that mattered. Now that I'd seen her, knew she was mine, I wanted to taste her, to sink my cock into her body and watch her eyes cloud with need. I'd agreed to the Brides Program's match, agreed to be her mate for life. I'd even agreed to the royal family's request that I share her with Rolf and Erik.

I'd vowed to care for her, protect her, and give her everything she needed. But I could not love her. Love would be left to Erik and Rolf. Love, for me, would be an impossible feat—but that did not mean I wanted harm to come to her. Not like Loren. The woman from Sector Two who I'd loved so long ago.

I'd loved her too much, allowed her every indulgence and she'd died for it. Drowned in a lake late one night with her friends. They hadn't watched her closely enough, lost her in the darkness. If I'd been there, she would have been protected, watched over. But no.

With Sophia, I would protect her with my life. Dominate her if need be, but not love. No, I couldn't love again. And yet, Sophia was mine. Just like Rolf and Erik were mine. Just like the three Kings and their lovely mate, Leah, were mine. Little Allayna, with her bouncing red curls and big blue eyes. Mine. I protected what was mine. Whoever had threatened our mate would die by my hand.

The transport technician looked to us as Erik cursed, shaking his head. "Their transport room confirmed no transport occurred. Sophia Antonelli is missing."

Lev moved to stand directly beside Erik and watched his fingers move over the display. If Lev knew how to use the machinery, he would have pushed the big warrior out of the way and done it himself. He had to stand by, like I did, helpless to find my mate.

"Were there any other transports occurring?" the King asked.

The technician frowned, his hands moving over the control station at a frantic pace. "Yes. One other."

Erik stood on the other side of the technician, his eyes narrowing as he, too, read the reports. Erik's eyes were serious, the color of storm clouds. Erik did not play the lighthearted Viken, as Rolf did. Nor did he feel the weight of the darkness as I. He walked in a cloud of gray, apathetic and detached from the world. I knew he'd lost his family, every single one of them, in a brutal attack. He'd never offered details, not in the ten years I'd fought by his side in the Hive war. He kept his dark secrets even when buried balls deep in a willing woman or neck deep in his cups, too drunk to stand.

He'd lost everything, as I had. Neither of us had anything to go home to. We didn't need to live a Sector life. The decision to stay at Viken United, to serve the new royal family, had been easy.

Rolf, on the other hand? I had no idea why Rolf did not return to Sector Three after we'd served our time in the Hive war. When Erik asked, Rolf shrugged and said he was afraid Erik and I would kill each other without him around to intervene. And so he'd remained with us as part of the royal guard.

"Erik, where the fuck is she? Can't you pull up her coordinates? Contact Earth. Surely they tracked her transport," I demanded.

"Hold onto your balls, boys. They covered their tracks," Erik insisted. I blinked slowly and held myself in check. Erik's words were in jest, but Sophia was his mate, and I recognized the look in his eyes now.

Murderous. Which was a perfect reflection for the rage coursing through my veins.

"They?" I asked.

"Who is they?" the King asked. "Have you confirmed it's the VSS?"

I cursed and resumed pacing as Leah and the baby moved to stand beside Lev once more. Clearly shaken, she reached to him for comfort, for strength. The sight made me burn with rage.

Somewhere out there, my mate was scared. Alone. Afraid.

And I couldn't reach her.

"Fuck this, Erik. Find her. Now."

Rolf grunted in agreement as Lev watched Erik's hands fly over the complex controls. Danger lurked in every shadow of late. For two thousand years before Lev's family had united the planet, the three sectors had been governed by whomever was the most powerful, the most ruthless. The Viken Sector Separatists preferred the old ways, the old system. They'd started the civil war three decades ago that killed our King and left the triplet princes orphans. Now that the brothers were united as one, and their young daughter, Allayna, was the recognized heir and ruler of the entire planet, the VSS had redoubled their efforts to eliminate the entire royal family once more.

Without the three kings, without Princess Allayna, there would be no clear line of ascension to the throne. It would be chaos. War.

Which was exactly what these bastards wanted.

The young princess's approaching first birthday celebration served as a blatant reminder of all those powerful families had lost. The enthusiastic outpouring of love from the entire planet's population for the adorable little princess had increased the separatists' recruitment efforts, for the princess was the true unifier of Viken. Every day new protests arose in one of the sectors, clashes between Viken United warriors and those still loyal to the individual sector leaders. Most of their loyalty bought with coin, or paid for in blood.

The three kings of Viken, each raised in one of the sectors after being orphaned as young boys, had begun the process of uniting the planet. The birth of their daughter had solidified their hold on the throne even more. But those unwilling to give up power hid like monsters in the dark, waiting to strike.

As royal guards on Viken United, Rolf, Erik and I served the royal family with utmost loyalty. So far, the royal guard had managed to avert every attack on the royal family.

Until today.

Today, they'd tried to take the Queen, but stolen my mate instead.

"I've got her coordinates. Sophia did, indeed, arrive on Viken." Erik lifted his gaze to mine and I barely suppressed a growl. I did not know our Sophia, had yet to hold her, touch her, fuck her. But she was mine. And no one fucked with what belonged to me. I focused on my anger. If I thought about our little mate alone and scared, or worse, suffering, I'd lose my fucking mind.

"Where is she?" My voice was as cold as the pale metal of the sword on Rolf's back.

Erik raised his head, his blue eyes so dark they looked black. "The wilds."

"The wilds?" I ran my hand over the back of my neck.

Queen Leah gasped. "But, there's no transport pad in the wilds. The VSS destroyed it months ago."

Rolf looked around the frantic technician at Erik. "Well, he's right." He pointed at the glowing display. "These coordinates are in the wilds."

"Are you fucking telling me that the separatists kidnapped our mate, mid-transport?" This was a new security threat more serious than any previously faced.

Lev growled at the technician. "Get your fucking commander down here and figure out how they did it."

"Yes, sir." The technician opened communication to someone we could not see, but I ignored him.

"Get me there, Erik. Now."

The King held up a hand to stall me. "You don't know what you're transporting into. Let's summon more warriors to accompany you." He looked me up and down, quickly doing the same to both Rolf and Erik. His brow arched as he noticed the light armor we wore. We were expecting to greet a beautiful new mate, not go into battle. "You need armor and weapons. And more warriors."

"I'm not waiting. Our mate is out there, alone and scared. Don't ask me to wait."

The King scowled, but it was Queen Leah who won him to our side. "Lev. Let Gunnar handle it. Please. What would you do if it were me and Allayna out there in the wilds?" Queen Leah placed her hand over his heart and leaned into him.

I saw the moment he changed his mind. "All right. But they were after the Queen. I know you want to gut them, but we need them alive for questioning." He looked down at his mate and lifted his hand to lightly run his fingers over the soft, downy curls of his infant daughter. "It's time to force these bastards out of hiding."

"Understood." I wanted to kill the men who'd dared threaten what was mine, but I agreed. I'd take them alive, if I could, and let the interrogators have them.

Leah tugged at the King's hand and carried the princess onto the transport pad with her mate following behind. "We have to attend the peace negotiations, Lev. We must go. If you don't show up, the Sectors will start talking. They'll use it against us."

Lev gently kissed the top of her head, but his body vibrated with anger and frustration at unanswered questions. His female had been in danger—still could be —and he could not resolve it himself.

"You're right." Our King lifted his gaze to mine, one warrior from Sector Two demanding full vengeance from another. "Take care of this. Find your mate. Claim her. Make her safe."

"We will."

"And bring these spineless cowards to me," he said.

The princess tugged on her father's shirt with her chubby fingers and the gentleness of his touch belied the violence of his words.

"Yes, sir." I'd hunt down every single Viken who was involved in the kidnapping, not only because our King demanded it, and not because they'd threatened the Queen's life, but because they'd taken what was mine. My mate.

Lev ordered the technician to transport them back to Sector Three. The King, Queen and Allayna disappeared moments later, the silence in the transporter room deafening.

"Confirm their arrival at the Sector transport center," Rolf commanded.

The technician swiped the display a few times, then we heard Lev's voice. "We arrived safely. Find your mate."

He ended the connection without signing off. What more was there for him to say? We could not delay. While the Queen and princess were safe, the same could not be said for our mate. She was in the fucking wilds. Alone. No protection.

Erik and Rolf both turned to me. I was the highest-ranking officer among us, and more, I needed to be in control like I needed to breathe. The need to command was like an infection in my blood. "If our mate is in the wilds, then the transport pad has not been destroyed. The separatists put out false information," I said.

The technician looked confused.

"As soon as we're gone, find out who signed the fucking report."

"Yes, sir." I saw realization dawn in the young man's eyes and behind it, rage. Good. He was young, but loyal. He would take the threat to his Queen and the princess very seriously.

Erik nodded. "The transport station at those coordinates is still operational and receiving."

"Are you both fully armed?" I asked, inspecting my friends and fellow warriors.

Erik scoffed at me, as if the question were idiotic. It was. We never went anywhere these days without our weapons.

I nodded at them and we stepped up onto the transport pad. "Let's go get our mate."

SOPHIA

I HAD NO IDEA HOW LONG I WALKED THROUGH THE WOODS. At first, I'd run. Then I'd stumbled over the rough undergrowth and tripped over the stupid dress. I hadn't heard anyone following me and so I slowed. Besides, the stitch in my side wasn't going away and it only reminded me that I rarely hit the gym. Animals were around. I could hear them, see a few small ones scurry off.

With the thick forest cover, there was no direct sunlight. Or suns? How many did Viken have? It wasn't cold, in fact, I was sweating in my heavy dress. I came to a stream and knelt beside it, cupped the cool water in my hands and drank. I'd probably get some kind of funky parasite, but I wasn't going to die of thirst. And thank God, the water tasted like...well...water. The knees of my dress became damp and stuck to me, clinging to my legs and weighing me down when I stood.

I undid the buttons and shrugged off the heavy, cumbersome garment. Beneath, I wore a simple white slip that fell to just above my knees. It wasn't any more revealing than a short sundress on Earth. Tugging at the scooped neckline, I peeked beneath and saw that I wore something halfway between a corset and a bra. My girls were well contained and didn't bounce around, so I was thankful. Leaving the dress behind, I continued walking, following the edge of the stream. The shoes I wore were simple and flat. I didn't know what would happen to them if they got wet, so I stuck to the dry bank and didn't feel the need to cross.

The sun did not seem to set in Viken, nor move across the sky. It felt like hours since I'd killed that man, miles I'd walked from the transport building and I had seen no one, heard no one other than the little tree creatures. I felt like fucking Snow White walking through the forest, waiting for the woodsman to come cut out my heart.

Did anyone even know I was here? That I'd gone missing? Or been rerouted. Or whatever the hell had happened.

My legs ached, the muscles shaking and I was hungry. The last thing I'd eaten on Earth had been hours before my testing at the bride center. Who knew how long ago that was? My stomach thought it had been days and days, the ache sharp as a knife. I'd been told that Earth was light years away from this planet, so I was allowed to grumble about wanting a hamburger and french fries. I'd earned a damn double-fudge milkshake with whipped cream and little chocolate chips, even if it would stick to my ass.

Nauseous and dizzy, I couldn't keep going. I needed to rest. Moving away from the stream, I turned back into the woods until I found a large tree and began to climb, wedging myself into a seat of sorts made where three large branches intersected. Pulling my knees up beside me, I leaned my head against the smooth bark and slowed my breathing. Glad that it wasn't cold, I rested for several minutes as the noise of the forest resumed around me. Birds sang songs I did not recognize. A strange, fuzzy black creature hopped from branch to branch like a squirrel back home. Odd insects flew in the air around me, but most left me alone. One or two landed on me, but I quickly waved them away, wishing I'd kept the blue dress for a blanket or bug net.

At least I hadn't tripped over it for the past few miles.

"Sophia!"

The loud cry caused me to stiffen, but I did not respond as three large Viken males entered the woods directly below me. The man who'd cried out was tall and blond, his eyes too far away to see clearly, I suspected they were green. He was big and muscular, his large frame covered in a dark green uniform with a red band around his arm. His face was handsome enough to cause my heart to race with more than fear.

"Sophia!" A second man walked a few paces behind the blond and called out to me as well. He turned his head from side to side, looking for me. He was thicker of chest and a few inches shorter than his companion. But he looked like my favorite actor, his long brown hair tied at the base of his skull to flow midway down his back. He wore a brown uniform with the same red band around his arm and carried a strange-looking weapon he used to push aside foliage in his search for me.

Allowing them to pass, I sat in silence for long minutes and considered coming down from the tree as they wandered farther and farther away from my position. I'd begun to think I should climb down and take my chances that they weren't here to kill me. That was, until I saw the third man.

He did not speak as he followed at least a quarter mile behind them. He moved through the woods on silent feet, his dark gaze searching everything.

Of the three, he was the only one to look up.

45

Shrinking back behind the huge tree's main trunk, I hid completely and peeked down at him through a full spray of emerald green leaves. He wore black from head to toe with the same red armband. He had dark black hair, cut short and dark eyes. His face reminded me of the hottest Greek or Italian model ever to grace the pages of a magazine, but his skin was darker, the color of my favorite mocha latte. He was beautiful, but hard. It was his eyes that held me frozen in place. They were cold, unemotional and calculating as he followed the others through the woods.

So, the first two were meant to flush me out for the hunter following behind.

I might be a city girl, but I wasn't stupid. I'd seen this scenario played out on the streets back home. Send a couple guys around to knock on doors and stir up trouble. And, just when everyone thought it was safe, the real enforcer showed up and knocked someone's teeth in.

Nope. Not falling for this bullshit.

4

THE LAST MAN WALKED DIRECTLY BENEATH ME AND I HELD my breath, not daring to make so much as a whisper of sound as he stopped moving. Heart pounding so loudly I feared he would hear it, I clutched at the tree and prayed he would just keep going. If he looked up, straight up, I'd be his.

The weapon in his hand, a larger version of the space gun I'd held earlier—the gun I'd used to kill—rested across his arm like a familiar friend. The dark black sleeves of his uniform inched up and I bit my lip to keep the scream trapped in my throat as I spotted the tattoo on the inside of his wrist.

The three-headed serpent.

Fuck.

That answered that. The transporter guy must have sent these three to finish me off.

I closed my eyes, the air I'd held trapped in my lungs burning like acid.

With a slow, controlled technique I'd learned in yoga class, I released a small trickle of air before filling my lungs in the same manner.

I counted to a hundred. Two hundred. Three. When I opened my eyes he was still there.

I wanted to scream at him to move on, to get the hell out of here.

The other two returned to join him, their calls increasing in volume as they came nearer.

"Gunnar? What are you doing? We have to keep moving." The blond one spoke.

Gunnar. So, my tattooed hunter had a name.

Gunnar shook his head slowly and raised his hand to silence his companions. "She's here. I can feel it."

The man with long brown hair slung his gun across his back on a long strap and frowned. "Not this again."

The blond laughed. "Shut up, Erik. We've already established that Gunnar's instincts are solid. Saved your ass more than once."

Erik shook his head, clearly impatient. "Come on, Gunnar. If she were here, she would have come out by now."

No.

"No." Gunnar said the word as I thought it. "She will be frightened and confused. You saw the dead man."

"Fuck. You really think she killed him?" Erik asked.

Gunnar didn't respond, his gaze wandering the woods. The trees. Getting too damn close. The guy was

48

fucking intense, and scary as hell. And so gorgeous he should come with a warning label. The intense attraction I felt for him made me burn with rage. Was this how the Vikens played? Send an assassin to seduce you with intense good looks before he ripped your throat out?

I rolled my eyes at my own theatrics. But, seriously, these guys could give the Corellis a run for their money.

And really, who had lackeys this damn gorgeous? All three of them were walking, talking sex gods, their tight uniforms stretched over thick, muscled chests. How was I supposed to fight them once they found me? How was I going to survive? I didn't know anyone on this planet. I had no food, no money, no weapons, no cell phone, and no one to call if I did.

And these men were huge, toting guns, and determined to find me. I was so screwed.

A great big case of feel-sorry-for-myself rolled through me and tears gathered in my eyes. I tilted my head to make sure they simply ran down my cheeks, rather than fall on one of the hunters' heads. If I wanted to deal with this kind of stress, I could have stayed on Earth and tried to feel pretty in the bright orange prison jumpsuit.

But at least I'd be alive. I could sit in a cozy jail cell, read about a thousand books, and try not to get my ass kicked a couple times a week. For twenty-five years.

How sad that jail now seemed like it may have been the wiser choice. Because, as of right now, the odds of survival weren't looking like they were in my favor.

Gunnar tilted his head to the side, as if he could hear me thinking. The man was freaking me out.

Erik looked at the blond. "Well, Rolf? What now? You know he's not going to fucking move."

Rolf studied both men in silence before offering his opinion. "If Gunnar's right, then she's hiding from us."

Gunnar snorted. "Got a gift for deductive reasoning, there, genius?"

Rolf slung his own weapon across his back. And for some reason, the fact that only one man was still ready to shoot me on sight, instead of three, made my shoulders sag in relief. Gunnar was scary, but I'd met more than a few men like him. Cold. Hard. Ruthless. He wouldn't be trigger happy, and he wouldn't lose his cool. The other two seemed more like loose cannons.

Rolf shrugged. "All right. Gunnar's never wrong."

"Fuck. I know that. But what do we do about it?" Erik of the long brown hair asked.

Gunnar walked to the base of the tree where I hid and settled his back against it. "We get the Queen out here. Sophia's not going to believe anything we say. Maybe she'll listen to one of her own."

———

ROLF

GUNNAR WAS TOO CALM. I'D RARELY SEEN HIM THIS relaxed, and never when we were on so important a mission. In the transporter room, when it was discovered Sophia had been transported intentionally to the wilds, I saw a tick in his jaw, his fists clench. He didn't lose control. Ever. But the intensity he wore like a second skin had faded, confusing me. Why was he so fucking calm?

True, Gunnar wasn't keen on a mate, but he'd accepted the arrangement. I expected neither he nor Erik would ever fall over themselves for our matched bride—like Lev had been when he'd gotten his mate and daughter in his hands after the mistaken transport—but love her or not, they were possessive fucks. If Sophia was ours, both would see her safe, see her cared for. Protected. Cherished even. But love? Not happening.

But knowing that our Sophia was lost in the fucking wilds made Gunnar frantic in his own, quiet way. His calm was deceiving to many an enemy, causing them to relax a fraction of a second before Gunnar went for the kill. But now, in the wilds, Gunnar didn't even seem concerned for our mate.

Gunnar sat on the ground, his back leaning against the tree and his ion blaster across his lap. He nodded at Erik and me. "You two, set up a perimeter around me while we wait for the Queen."

I caught Erik's eye, who shrugged and moved to Gunnar's left, farther up the trail we'd been following, but remaining in sight. For a minute or two, I stood, confused. What the hell was going on?

"Gunnar, we should keep moving," I advised. "I know you didn't want a mate, but this is not the time..."

"Of course, I want her." Gunnar practically barked at me, his calm façade cracking. But this was the first time I'd ever heard such a statement from him. His odd behavior concerned me, for the three of us were her mates together. We'd all been matched to her. Without Gunnar, the match would not be complete.

Gunnar used his blaster to indicate I should head to his left, opposite Erik, and set up a true perimeter guard around him and the damn tree.

I arched a brow and squatted down before him to argue. His dark eyes met mine. Held. Then shifted up.

I'd been blind to what my friend *wasn't* saying.

My shoulders relaxed. Sophia *was* here. Above us. Gunnar hadn't given up, he was protecting her. What Earth woman, who'd transported into fuck-knows-what, been attacked and forced to kill a man before running off, alone, into the woods, would come out of hiding for three Viken hulks like us? If Gunnar pulled her from the tree, she'd be afraid of us, terrified even, and wouldn't be calm enough to sense our connection. Our bond.

If she was afraid of us, we'd never be able to make her truly ours.

And so we'd go about it another way. We were more blast-and-grab or shock-and-awe kinds of warriors. This *calm* approach was almost unnerving, but our quarry had never been a mated female before. *Our* mate.

"Erik, call the kings," I said. "Get Queen Leah here. She's from Earth. Our mate will trust her."

Erik's eyebrows winged up at my agreement with Gunnar, but he only nodded and spoke into the InterCom on his wrist, coordinating with Lev and offering our exact coordinates for them to travel to after transport. "Bring guards with you, the transport center is not secure," he said before signing off.

We were the only ones out here, but there was a dead man outside the transport center to prove that evil lurked.

"I estimate twenty minutes until their arrival," Erik said.

We had walked quite a distance tracking Sophia, but we'd turned several times and ended up parallel to the transport station. With the coordinates in advance, the others would take the direct route we had not.

"Our mate, I believe she will be a handful," Gunnar commented, looking down at his fingernails.

Erik frowned and I walked a few feet in the opposite direction to watch the trail behind us. "Oh? She looked beautiful in the testing image, not difficult," I countered. "Her hair looked soft to touch. Her skin smooth. I, for one, can't wait to find her, difficult or not."

"Not difficult," Gunnar clarified. "A handful. Courageous. Fierce. Determined. Passionate. If she is matched to us, she will not be meek." He grunted. "I do not want meek."

No, I knew he didn't. However, submissive was quite different. "I doubt she'll be meek, Gunnar. She was convicted of smuggling, after all. Our lady is a pirate."

Erik laughed. "Oh yes. According to her profile, she was very busy breaking Earth's laws before her transport. I can't wait to feel all that rebellious fire riding my cock."

Gunnar raised a brow. "Her past is irrelevant. She's ours now. If she believes she can get away with such rebellion here, she'll earn a place over my knee."

Erik's humor erupted in rapid-fire speech. "You'll take her over your knee regardless, Gunnar." He lifted his weapon so the barrel rested against his shoulder, pointed to the sky.

Gunnar grinned at me. "No. Spanking her pretty little ass will be Erik's pleasure."

Fuck. My cock grew hard at the thought. I hoped she misbehaved, challenged us. Often. I knew Erik would pet her naked ass and plunge his fingers into her wet pussy as he made her bottom burn. If I were lucky, she'd have her mouth around my cock as he did it.

I watched Erik for a moment before laughing. "Well, since she's been matched to all three of us, no doubt she'll want it as much as he does." And she'd want my dirty words filling her ears as he did it, as we took her, fucked her, filled her and made her ours forever.

"If she's anything like the Queen, she'll be perfect," I said, and decided to maintain my watch, but from a comfortable position as well. I leaned back against a tree a few feet from Gunnar and crossed my ankles.

Erik looked at me as if I were crazy. Perhaps I was, since I was desperate to get Sophia into my arms and fuck her, just like the dream I'd had during the matching protocols. And then some.

Gunnar loved control. Erik loved public discipline and had a particular obsession with the feminine ass. Me? I wanted to mind fuck our little mate. I wanted her head as tangled up with our cocks as her heart. The bonding essence in our seed would ensure she wanted us, needed our touch. But that wasn't enough for me. I wanted more. I wanted her mind as well as her body.

Noticing the confusion on Erik's face, I flicked my gaze up high into the tree, just as Gunnar had for me.

"You Sector One men love to show off your mates. Don't you, Erik? You probably want to walk her naked through the courtyards, settle her on her knees, spank her and fuck her with all of Viken United watching," I said.

Erik glanced to Gunnar, still at ease at the base of the tree. It took him a few seconds, but he caught on. Sighed. "Gods, yes. Stripped bare, she will come awake beneath our hands as a crowd gathers to admire her body. Her nipples will tighten into hard little pebbles and her pussy will weep with desire as Gunnar holds her hands behind her back. Rolf, you'll have your head between her thighs, feasting on all that sweetness. I'll adorn her nipples with clamps, with little gems dangling from them. You'll tongue her until she begs, but she'll wait for permission to come."

Gunnar grunted approval, his free hand adjusting the large bulge in his pants. "I'll make sure she is mindless with pleasure before I let her come."

Erik agreed. "And when she does, I'll fill her ass with my cock."

Gunnar grunted at Erik's story. My cock hardened at the thought of getting my mouth on her perfect pussy.

"She might come from Rolf's mouth on her pussy," Gunnar added. "But one orgasm won't be enough for our mate. We know she needs more. One man won't push her body as she'd need. No, she'll need all of us."

Erik shifted his cock in his pants. "Our mate will love it when we take her."

"Everywhere," I added. I looked at Gunnar, who looked nearly asleep he was so relaxed. I knew it was an act, meant to soothe our frightened mate.

"And everyone will see how beautiful she is, how she responds to her mates, how she comes when we command. Everyone will be envious of us," Erik added. The man was an exhibitionist and would all but flaunt Sophia, taunting every warrior at Viken United, and anywhere else, with what they couldn't have. He'd *show*, but not *share*.

"And what of our seed power?" I asked. "No Viken woman can bond to three men."

Gunnar shook his head. "No. A Viken woman would not. But Sophia is human, like our Queen. She is ours. And like our Queen, she will accept seed from all three of us. Bond to all three of us."

"Gods, she'll be insatiable," I added.

"I won't complain if she can't keep her hands off me," Erik added.

"Nor I," Gunnar said.

It was becoming too painful to continue this line of conversation. All I wanted to do was pull out my cock and jerk off. But I would save my seed, save my orgasm for when I was deep inside Sophia's pussy. My pleasure belonged to her, just as hers did to me. To all three of us.

Just then, we heard voices calling our names.

They weren't being stealthy, their footfalls heavy and the underbrush rustled as they moved.

"Over here!" Gunnar called, rising to his feet.

Soon enough, Lev and Leah stood before us, surrounded by a host of a half dozen royal guards dressed as we were, in full military uniform with red bands around their arms to signify their service to Viken United, to our three kings and their beloved mate and daughter.

We bowed, but Leah wasn't in the mindset of a queen, but of an impatient woman.

"Where is she?" she asked. "Is she hurt?"

"I do not know her condition, my Queen. I suspect she is terrified and would not have come down without you here, a friend from Earth, to reassure her." Gunnar pointed up and everyone's heads lifted. I'd avoided even glancing in that direction for fear Sophia would know she'd been discovered and panic.

Leah squinted for a moment, then gasped. "Sophia? Oh, sweetie, what are you doing up there?"

We could only see the side of our mate's face, the rest of her hidden behind the huge trunk of the tree. Panic at the thought of her falling from such a height had me stepping closer to the base. I was glad I hadn't looked up before now, otherwise I would have climbed the tree and saved her.

Her hair was long and golden and her eyes were wide and fearful. In just her slip, her skin was creamy and smooth, just like Queen Leah's. And she was small. So very small. How had she fought against the dead man...and won?

Gunnar was right. Our mate was far from meek. And she did not look impressed with the small army of Viken warriors below her. Leah was the only female among us, the only one our mate might trust.

5

Sophia didn't move, didn't even blink as the Queen shouted up into the tree.

"Listen, Sophia. I know you're from New York. Antonelli? Italian, right? I'm Leah Adams, from Miami. I'm from Earth, too. I walked away from cheeseburgers and bad TV to come here. Actually, I had an abusive and controlling asshole fiancé. Perhaps Warden Egara mentioned me after your testing? I was the first mate matched to Viken and I got the three kings. They're identical triplets." She angled her head to Lev. "They're all hot like him."

She paused, let the words sink in. Sophia did not respond. Leah stepped forward and held her hands out at her sides, imploring our mate to come down.

"Your mates are here. They were frantic for you. They

found you and they've been sitting here, guarding you. Waiting for me to introduce you. Don't be afraid of them. They're the good guys, I promise. You can come down now. They'll protect you. No matter what happened after your transport, you're safe. Gunnar, Erik and Rolf are your matched mates."

I moved to stand beside Gunnar and Erik so Sophia could see the three of us together.

"Yes, they're big brutes," Leah continued, huffing out a laugh. "But they're yours. They won't hurt you. Right, guys?"

We nodded in unison and watched as Leah scooted around the trunk. Sophia sat there, her fingers gripping the rough bark. She looked at each of us in turn, and my cock grew hard as she looked into my eyes for the first time. I saw longing there, and fear. Her gaze lingered on Erik's long brown hair before shifting to Gunnar.

She froze and her eyes widened, growing darker, but not with fear. I'd seen many women react to Gunnar in exactly the same way. With desire.

"Come down, sweetie. I promise you, you're safe now," Leah insisted, her voice soothing.

Gunnar handed me his ion blaster, stepped forward and held out his hand to our mate. "Come down now, Sophia. You're safe. I am Gunnar, your mate. And I give you my solemn vow, no one will ever hurt you again."

We waited. Impatiently.

"I...can't." Sophia's voice was soft, timid. Tired. The small sound made my heart clench in my chest.

"They won't hurt you," Leah repeated. "No one here will hurt you. If I know your mates, no one will hurt you ever again."

I heard Gunnar grunt.

"I'm not afraid of you, at least not anymore," Sophia continued, and she stared down into Gunnar's upturned face. "I can't climb down. My muscles are frozen and stiff. I'll fall."

I didn't wait then, but stalked over to the base of the tree and began to climb. Sophia's eyes widened the closer I got to her, but she didn't move. When I stood on a lower branch and we were at eye level with each other, I smiled.

"Hello, beautiful. I'm Rolf, your mate."

She offered a small smile. Gods, she was lovely. This close I saw that her hair was actually a mix of colors, light brown and red strands mixed in with the masses of gold. Her skin was soft and creamy, the swells of her breasts visible beneath the thin slip of cloth she wore. Her lips were a pale pink and her soft brown eyes looked up at me with a stark loneliness I understood all too well. When I held out my hand, she placed her smaller one in mine and that slight touch made me burn to taste her, to wrap her in my arms and keep her safe from the world. The heat of it, the *connection*, had her meeting my gaze, wide eyed.

Nodding once, perhaps telling her that I felt it, too, I then glanced down at the others, a good twenty feet below. No wonder she was scared. She was a tiny thing and had a crowd of big men beneath her. And a long way to fall.

"You've had quite the day. What do you say I help you from this tree and we go far, far from here? Where there's a bath and food. Some clean clothes. Gunnar and Erik want to meet you, too." I was the soother of the three of us. I'd never appreciated that mantle before, but now, I was thrilled. I would be the one to coax our mate into my arms, into *our* protection, once and for all.

"All right."

Her hand was so small in mine, I could not wait to discover what I would feel pressing her body to mine, tasting her. Thrusting my cock into her eager core and listening to her soft cries of pleasure.

First, I had to see her safe. Usually everyone else took care of the big problems. I was the lighthearted one. Joking, inserting humor into desolate situations. Of course I wasn't always so upbeat. Hell, that fun banter hid the fucking hurt I carried around. But this, Sophia, was bigger than stupid hurt from my past. Bigger than my mother and my brother, the pain they'd caused me. What I hid behind a quick smile and a joke.

But our mate had been forced to defend herself, in the wilds. She hid from us as if we were a danger to her. And now, I used my quick smile and soft tone not to hide anything, but to relieve her worries. I was showing her the real me, because hell, she was mine.

I asked her to shift close enough that I could scoop her up into my arms. She was soft and warm and so tiny I didn't want to let her go. But I couldn't jump from this height holding her, so I had to set her on her feet beside me. I moved down branch by branch, holding her hand as she followed.

Erik stepped up and he held out his hands. "Jump, Sophia. I'll catch you."

She was directly above him, not more than a few feet. She reached her hands out and put them in his, then jumped. He caught her easily and she was in his tight hold. Erik would not let her go.

I lowered myself down to the soft forest floor and sighed, relieved to know we had our mate once and for all. Sophia buried her face in Erik's neck, all but burrowing in. He reveled in the embrace, squeezing her as tightly as he could without hurting her, then kissing the top of her head.

"Welcome to Viken, Sophia," Leah said.

Our mate turned her head and offered the Queen a small smile. "Yeah, well, it sucks so far," she muttered. "And I thought New York was bad."

Leah laughed. "I'm sure your mates will more than make it up to you." She wiggled her eyebrows at Sophia, who blushed a pretty shade of pink. Confused, I tilted my head at our Queen, unsure if I'd understood her suggestive tone.

"Leah, behave yourself," Lev commanded his mate, but the Queen threw back her head and laughed, the sound full of contagious happiness. Sophia's smile was genuine now. Even Lev, our stern-faced King, grinned at his joyful little mate.

But when Gunnar stepped close, Sophia's eyes widened and she pushed away, trying to escape Erik's arms. When he refused to let her go, she turned away, hiding her face. "No. Not him. If you're my mate, then don't let him touch me. I...don't trust him. You can't trust him."

The mood of the group changed then. Stilled. Even the animals in the woods seemed to sense something and were quiet. Erik offered a confused glance to Gunnar over Sophia's head. "Love, Gunnar might be a little moody and definitely intimidating, but I swear, he will not harm you."

She shook her head in refusal. "No. He has you all fooled."

I stepped in front of Gunnar and stroked over Sophia's hair. "Look at me, mate." I waited patiently as she turned her head and her dark, worried gaze met mine.

"Why are you so afraid? I have fought beside Gunnar in many battles, trusted him with my life. He is an honorable warrior and worthy mate. He is strong and will protect you with his life. If he were anything less, King Lev would not allow his mate, the Queen of Viken in his presence. *I* would not allow you to be near him."

Gunnar was just as Erik said. Intimidating. Moody as hell. He did not show his emotions, but I knew that Sophia's rejection of him was taking a toll.

"The man who attacked me had the same tattoo," she murmured. "He's a bad guy, working for them. He has you all fooled."

"Tattoo?" Lev asked.

Leah crossed her arms and scowled in Gunnar's direction. "A tattoo is an Earth term for a mark permanently etched into the skin with ink," she clarified. "Sometimes they are a personal choice, body art. Earth soldiers use them to identify with a certain branch of service. But many criminals and gangs use tattoos to identify themselves to one another as well." Leah looked up at Lev. "Do you use tattoos to indicate military service? Or ranks? Anything like that?"

"No, mate, we do not." Lev pushed the Queen behind him, protecting her from Gunnar.

The guards who had accompanied the King and Queen closed in on Gunnar, raising their weapons to keep him at bay. I looked at Erik, confused. What the fuck was happening here?

I stepped between Gunnar and the nearest blaster, my hands up in the air. "Look. Everyone calm down until we get this sorted out. I trust Gunnar with my life. There has to be some kind of mistake."

Gunnar's hand came to rest on my shoulder and he squeezed in gratitude. "Thank you, Rolf. But I would know what frightens our mate."

"What tattoo, Sophia? Where is it on Gunnar?" Leah asked.

I stepped out of the way so she could see our friend, her mate. She pointed. "It's on the inside of his wrist."

Gunnar looked down, then pushed up his sleeve. "This is the only mark I have."

Sophia's eyes widened in obvious fear and distrust. "Yes, that's it. The three-headed serpent."

"The man you killed had this mark, Sophia?" Gunnar asked, his voice calm, but with a sharp bite.

She shook her head. "No. Not him. The other one."

Erik leaned down, his lips close to Sophia's ear as he held her. "What other one?"

Sophia shoved at Erik's arms, who finally relented and let her go. She stepped forward. Shaking, she held out her hand to Gunnar. He stared at her for a moment, before lifting the marked wrist to her.

She wrapped her hands around his wrist and turned the mark face up, tracing the outline with her finger.

Gunnar closed his eyes and I witnessed the shudder that passed through his body at her gentle first touch. I understood how he felt.

"The man I killed was a minion, nothing more," she

said. She had all our attentions. The King, the Queen, the guards were all in her thrall. But not for the reason I had once hoped, because we celebrated the arrival of our mate, but because she was speaking of evil. An evil that lurked on Viken that she knew nothing about, but had transported directly into. "The man with this mark was angry, and ordered the transport guy to kill me."

"Why?" Gunnar asked, his gaze burning into Sophia with raw lust as she continued to hold his wrist. She was completely unaware of his need for her. I tried to step forward, to intervene in the questioning, but Lev held up his hand, stopping me. The royal guards who accompanied the Queen stood around Gunnar in a loose circle, their ion blasters all aimed at Gunnar's head, waiting for a command.

The danger, and his mate's touch, seemed to spike Gunnar's lust. Crazy bastard. Shaking my head, I stepped back to stand next to Erik and watch events unfold. I had no doubt that Gunnar was innocent. He was my brother-in-arms. I'd trusted my life to him on more than one occasion. I would trust our mate with him now.

Sophia's gaze seemed far away, as if she were going into shock. "He was angry. He wanted the Queen and the baby. Not me. He worked for someone he called Vikter, someone in Central City. Is that a place here? When he realized their mistake, that I was sent by mistake, he ordered his minion to transport him back to the city. Then, kill me."

"And this man you speak of, had a mark like mine?" Gunnar asked.

She raised her face to meet his gaze. "Yes. What does it mean?"

Lev cleared his throat. "I'd like an answer to that question as well."

The guards surrounding Gunnar shifted, tightening their ring around my friend.

Gunnar held Sophia's gaze as he answered her. "This is the mark of a Master Dominant at Club Trinity in Central City."

Queen Leah gasped. "Club Trinity?"

Lev chuckled. "Ah, yes. I thought I'd seen that mark before." Lev looked at Gunnar as Leah playfully slapped him on the shoulder.

"Of course you have," she said, rolling her eyes.

Lev captured her hand in his and held it to his chest. "How many Masters are there?"

Gunnar shook his head. "I haven't been there in twelve years. But, I don't believe the club will have changed much."

"It's been there for three hundred years," Lev said.

"Exactly," Gunnar agreed. "And in all those years, there's never been more than two hundred Masters at any one time."

"Two hundred. I was hoping for a smaller number of potential targets." Lev pulled Leah into his arms but spoke to the guards. "It's all right, men. Lower your weapons."

Sophia looked around wildly as her protection disappeared. Slowly, Gunnar pulled her forward until she was pressed to his chest. She did not fight him. "On my honor, mate, I vow I will kill the man who dared hurt you."

"But?" Sophia turned her head to look at Leah with a question in her eyes.

Leah shrugged. "That tattoo is from a sex club in Central City."

"Sex club?" I watched Sophia's eyes widen and her cheeks turn a pretty shade of pink. She might have been surprised by the news, but she wasn't afraid of it. No, our mate was intrigued...

"That club's got nothing to do with the men who are trying to kill me," Leah insisted.

"Why...why not? How do you know?" Sophia asked.

"The tattoo might help us find the man you saw, but won't help us track down the leader of the VSS," Leah answered, although Sophia didn't look as if Leah's answer had clarified anything for her. "Nor is the mark considered a poor reflection on Gunnar."

"You're mine now, Sophia." Gunnar's words had Sophia turning to face him.

"What's the VSS and why do they want Leah dead?" She frowned. "I don't understand."

"Don't worry. You will." Gunnar lowered his mouth and claimed Sophia's lips in a display of blatant ownership that made me ache to step forward and join them.

———

SOPHIA

GUNNAR'S KISS MADE ME BURN. EVEN NOW, THREE HOURS later, I could taste his lips on mine, feel the strength of his arms as he'd held me trapped in his embrace.

I should have screamed or kicked or something.

Anything but what I did. Which was melt into his arms like a weak fool and open my mouth for his conquest.

And now? Now, I was in some kind of royal palace, surrounded by more servants than the freaking Queen of England. At least twenty women were in the bedchamber. Some cleaned, some decorated with flowers and candles until the room looked like a fairy tale in the making. I'd been soaked and fed, massaged and braided. My hair was in an elaborate set of braids and coils arranged with beautiful orange flowers. The rags I'd been wearing had been replaced with a long, beautiful gown the color of burnished copper. It draped over my body, hugging every curve as if it were made for me.

I looked like a princess. But the butterflies in my stomach would not stop fluttering about. And as the maids began to disappear, one by one, my anxiety rushed into my throat.

I knew what was coming. My three mates, who were eager to claim me. These women were making me perfumed and perfect for them.

For their taking.

Three mates. At the same freaking time.

Holy shit. What had I gotten myself into?

Even as the thought passed through my body with a shiver of panic, my pussy grew wet, my breasts heavy. Memories from the bride processing center swirled in my mind, but this time, I had names and faces to put on the men touching me, fucking me, bringing me pleasure.

I'd been matched to all three of them. It was unheard of on Earth. Sure, there were threesomes -- or foursomes -- but that was just sex. A bucket list item to check off. I hadn't even found one man I'd liked enough to keep around on Earth. But three? Forever?

I kept thinking that, over and over, as the women had worked on me as if I were a small child being dressed for a party.

Without doubt, each of my mates made my breath hitch and my pulse race. They were huge, handsome warriors. And soon, their complete attention would be on me.

I had survived the Corellis. I'd survived the transport mix-up and an asshole a foot taller and a hundred pounds heavier trying to kill me. I could survive wild, three-man sex with Viken warriors who worshipped my body, who wanted nothing more than to win my heart and bring me pleasure.

Assuming that was, indeed, what they wanted. With Rolf and Erik, I was fairly confident. But Gunnar frightened me on a fundamental level I could not explain. He made me nervous and unsure. And it wasn't just the tattoo on his wrist. No, it was the way he watched me, the way his gaze locked onto me like a predator's, with complete focus.

He looked at me like he owned me, could do anything he liked with my body. And as much as that scared me, it excited me, too. I was afraid of him, but even more afraid of myself. Because after that one kiss, I wasn't sure I would be able to refuse him anything. Anything at all. I wasn't even sure I wanted to.

Alone in my room, I walked to the balcony overlooking the royal gardens below. Leah had explained that this was the royal fortress at Viken United, an island stronghold straight out of a medieval tale of knights and fair maidens. The castle was massive, and this room and the apartment suite attached to it was now mine. Forever.

Leah assured me, even if I did not choose to accept my mates, if I were to reject the match and choose another, this place would be mine as long as I lived on Viken.

And since there was no going back to Earth, like ever, that assurance settled me more than I'd thought possible.

Having the Queen of an entire planet on my side was proving to be pretty damn nice. Earth girls stuck together, even if we weren't on Earth.

I walked to the chest-high rail and propped my arms on the edge. Below me, vast gardens spread in the center of the castle courtyard. Completely surrounded on all four sides, the gardens were the Queen's sanctuary. Trees and flowers similar to those I'd seen in the forest stretched out below. I was on the fourth floor and could trace the many trails and gathering places down below. It was no Central Park, but it was more than big enough to wander in for hours. To escape.

I felt them before I heard them, their presence behind me sending a shiver down my spine.

Taking a deep breath, I turned, placing my back to the railing, and inspected the three men who were now mine standing before me. Big, so big.

Rolf, with his golden hair and easy grin, leaned against the doorframe, wearing tight pants and leather of a dark green with furs lining his cloak to match. His chest was bare, draped only with the leather of his sword's scabbard where it hung over his back. Every muscle of his lean frame so well defined I could trace them with my tongue. His pants hung low on his hips and his abdomen looked like a washboard, the outline of the erection just below that made me gasp and I tore my gaze away.

Beside him stood Erik, his long brown hair let loose to hang around his shoulders like a rock star god. He wore a similar outfit, but a dark, chocolate brown. He, too, was bare chested and magnificent. Thicker than Rolf, his chest and shoulders were broad and muscled, massive. All too quickly did I remember the feel of being pressed to him in the forest when he'd held me. I could still smell his skin where I'd pressed my nose to his neck and breathed him in.

Shaking now, I turned to Gunnar, who stood with his head tilted and his arms crossed. He wore black. Of course, he was in fucking black. The dark color matched his hair and dark eyes, but unlike the others, he wore no cloak. His chest and shoulders were bare. Thick leather straps circled his wrists and arms, straps that appeared to have no purpose, but somehow made him even more virile.

Rolf stepped forward first, holding out his hand. "Are you ready, love?"

I shook my head and tried to step back, but I had nowhere to go. "Not exactly. You three are a bit intimidating all at once. I'm just an art dealer from New York City. Viken is a little... overwhelming. Like you."

Gunnar nodded. "Of course, we are. That is our job, to be intimidating. To everyone but you." He pointed at Erik. "You, inside. Rolf, let us know when she's ready."

Gunnar and Erik disappeared back into my room and I breathed a sigh of relief, until Rolf stepped forward and put his arms on either side of me, trapping me in place.

He leaned down until he was eye level with me, and I

could do nothing but stare into his pale gaze. Where Gunnar would most likely pin me down with rope or restraints, Rolf didn't need that. He just needed to look at me and I was enthralled.

"I want to kiss you, Sophia. I've been burning with envy at Gunnar's kiss for hours."

That made me laugh, made my nerves calm. Somehow, just a few words from him had me at ease. Had me feeling beautiful and desired. I licked my lips in anticipation as he lowered his to mine.

The kiss was nothing like Gunnar's instant domination. This kiss coaxed and explored. Where Gunnar was aggressive, hard, Rolf was gentle and reverent. I melted. My nerves shoved away as I wrapped my arms around his waist and kissed him back. He stepped forward, closed the small space between us and pressed me into the railing. There was no escaping him, not that I wanted to. Rolf's attentions were meant to soothe me, to ease me into the claiming. He was foreplay for what was to come.

The connection with Rolf did set me at ease, erased all my fears, all my worries. I had no idea what to do with three men, but they seemed to know what to do with me. I belonged to them and could easily be overwhelmed physically by all of them, but they'd known I needed space, needed coaxing. And with just the one kiss, I'd received it.

But so quickly, knowing Gunnar and Erik watched made me eager to tease them. I felt powerful and very feminine. And so when Rolf pulled back, I nodded.

I was ready.

Rolf lifted a black length of silk. "This is for your eyes, love."

I fought for air, so turned on by the idea of having that thick fabric over my eyes, my hands shook. "Why?"

He leaned down and nuzzled my neck first, then my ear. I angled my head to give him better access. "Because Gunnar said so."

I bit my lip, fighting the empty pulse of my core at his stark words.

Because Gunnar said so.

"Do you always do what Gunnar says?" I whispered, eyeing the blindfold.

He chuckled, his lips tracing up the line of my jaw. "No. But when it comes to you, mate, Erik and I are content to give Gunnar what he wants."

"And what does he want?"

Gunnar stepped out onto the balcony.

"You screaming in pleasure," he said. His voice was dark, his bearing dominant, but the look in his eyes was tender. Hot.

I gulped at the intensity.

"Do you want us, Sophia?"

I nodded immediately. I ached for more than just one kiss. And after the hell I'd been through the last few hours, hell, the last few months, I was more than ready to forget everything but pleasure. Even more, I needed to feel connection to another person, to be anchored. I felt like a piece of driftwood in the sea for so long now, since my mother's death. I had no immediate family, no business, no one to love.

Tears welled in my eyes and I looked away from the

man watching me with complete focus. But Rolf was having none of it. He lifted his hand to my cheek and turned me back to face him. "Why the tears? Are you afraid, love? Please don't be afraid. We would never hurt you."

"I know." I tried to smile, but knew the effort was wasted as his pale green eyes darkened in concern.

"Talk to me, Sophia. I am yours now. Tell me what troubles you."

I am yours now. The finality, the commitment in his words shocked me to my core in a way I'd not anticipated. I shook my head, unable to express the explosion of emotion welling up from inside. I'd been alone for so damn long. I leaned into his hand and let him wipe away my tear with the pad of his thumb. "It's stupid, Rolf. I've just been alone a really long time."

"Alone?" he asked.

"My mother getting sick, the Corellis who forced me to work for them. My mother dying. My job as an art dealer turning from something I loved into something I hated. That ultimately sent me to jail. Alone," I repeated.

"Well, you now have three very protective, dominant, obsessive mates. You might wish to be alone again soon enough." He spoke in jest, but there was a distant hurt in his eyes I would explore later. Right now, I just wanted to snap the thread of tension that had been building inside me for days. Waiting. Waiting. Waiting. I was so fucking tired of waiting, of being alone.

"I'm ready, Rolf. Tell them I'm ready." Hell yes, I was ready. Ready to be touched and held. Ready to believe that I'd never be alone again. Even if they didn't love me, they wanted me. They would protect me and make me burn with lust. For now, that was enough. I needed to forget all about Earth, and orange jumpsuits, the mafia and assholes trying to kill me.

"You're sure?"

I nodded and sucked his thumb into my mouth before running my tongue along the tip. "I don't want to think anymore, Rolf. I just want to feel."

Rolf kissed me, hard and fast before turning around to face the empty doorway behind which I knew my other two mates watched and waited. My nipples pebbled beneath the dress and I thrust my chest out as the heat of Rolf's chest warmed my back. He lifted the blindfold over my eyes and I allowed him to tie it. I blinked a few times, searching for a hint of light. Nothing.

I heard the others arrive as Rolf's hands slid to my shoulders, pushing the straps of my gown down onto my upper arms. I held absolutely still as multiple hands settled upon me, began undoing my dress, brushing over every inch of skin they quickly exposed. I stood like a statue of a Greek goddess and let them worship me with their touch. I didn't wonder who was touching me. Which man kissed along my bare shoulder. Whose hand slid down my spine. Whose palm cupped my breast. Whose mouth suckled at my nipple, or whose lips felt like phantom kisses on my thighs.

It didn't matter. They were all touching me.

They were all *mine.*

6

"YOU'RE SO BEAUTIFUL, SOPHIA," I MURMURED.

I would have to thank the head attendant at a much later time for the lack of undergarments, for as soon as the dress pooled at her feet, she was bare to us.

Gunnar growled at the sight of all her creamy skin, her lush curves.

"Perfection," whispered Rolf as he cupped her full breast, as if testing the weight of it.

With her eyes covered, we looked to her body for her responses, the way she arched her back into Rolf's touch, the gasp that escaped her lips, the flushing of her pale skin.

She was ours. How did we ever have doubts about this? About her?

We touched her gently, reverently, learning every silky

soft inch of her. As Rolf played with her breasts, made her nipples hard, Gunnar dropped to his knees and stroked up and down her shapely legs, kissed her hip, cupped her lush ass.

I licked and sucked at her shoulder, then along the tender line of her neck, found the sweet spot behind her ear that made her sigh. When I felt her racing pulse beneath my lips, my cock pulsed. Throbbing against the front of my pants, I opened them and pulled my cock free. Gripped the base and stroked up to the tip, coaxing a slick drop of my essence to coat my fingertips. All the while, I kissed and nipped her flesh. Took her pert nipple into my mouth and sucked the hard tip deep.

When I felt the telltale wetness on my fingertips, I raised my hand to paint my seed to her other nipple and leaned forward to claim a kiss. I was the only one not to have kissed our mate, and I was tired of waiting.

The bonding essence in my seed hit her bloodstream as my tongue thrust deeply into her mouth. I'd given her just a hint of my need. All at once, she moaned and she... softened. There was no other word for the way her muscles relaxed, her skin warmed beneath our touch, her breathing lost its rhythm.

I glanced at Rolf over her shoulder and he, too, had his cock free. He was circling his fluid onto the long, elegant lines of her neck, up and down over her frantic pulse and I could see the way his essence seeped into her skin, her body taking it in as would a flower with water in a parched desert.

"Oh," she gasped. With her eyes closed, she didn't know that we were marking her with pre-cum, preparing her even further for our domination, with the first taste of our seed power. The bonding essence in our seed would alter her body on a cellular level, make her hunger for our touch, as we would for hers. The seed power kept newly bonded Viken couples together through hardship. But, as we'd learned with Queen Leah, Earth women responded with a much more aggressive manner. The Queen had become addicted to her men, needed constant attention and actually been in pain without their bonding essence. The strongest effects lasted just a few weeks, and I had dreaded this time before I saw our mate.

Before I tasted her. Now, I could not wait to spend the next few weeks at her beckoning. If she needed to be fucked, stroked, pleasured, I was more than happy to comply.

In Sector One, where I'd been raised, it was common for newly mated couples to display their passionate connection in front of others. I'd always thought the men, with their public claiming, had lost their minds. Only now, as I tasted Sophia's kiss, captured her soft moan with my mouth and rubbed my essence into her creamy flesh did I understand. I longed to march her to the courtyard below and fuck her like a rutting stallion, force everyone in the fortress to listen to her scream her pleasure and see how beautiful she was. Pleasure that I'd given her.

My pleasure.

Sophia lifted her hand to my head and buried her hands in my hair, holding me close with her own demand. I knew her other hand had lowered to Gunnar's head, to the lips so very close to the pussy we would all soon claim.

We hadn't yet touched her core, although Gunnar's mouth was just inches away. He just needed to move his head and he'd be able to flick his tongue out and lick her. To taste her arousal, which I could see glistening on her thighs.

Gunnar's thoughts were the same as mine, for he spoke as he undid his own pants and took his cock in hand.

"I smell your need, Sophia. Dark and musky. Sweet, too. I want to taste you. We all do. Do you feel the power of our need?"

With his own pre-cum coating his fingers, he stroked between her thighs. From my position, I couldn't see more than his hand disappearing, but when she leaned back against Rolf and cried out, I knew Gunnar was touching her. More pre-cum streamed from my own cock at the sight of her open-mouthed cry, her flushed skin.

"That's it, Sophia. Do you feel our essence in your blood?"

"Yes." She arched her back and shifted her hips toward Gunnar. His hair was too short for her to command with just one hand. She pulled my head back down for another kiss as Gunnar continued to touch her wet core. Rolf's sweet words covered all of us as he held her still for our attention.

"We have a bond so powerful it connected us from across the universe. Our seed contains bonding elements that will make you crave our touch, mate. The fire in your blood will spread and burn through you until you come all over our cocks, over and over again."

She whimpered into my mouth and I rubbed more of my essence onto her nipple, pinching her as I felt her legs collapse. Rolf held her steady, his voice wrapping our mate in a sensual cocoon as Gunnar and I worked her body with our hands. "You can feel how much we want you. Fuck, how much we need you."

Sophia didn't release me, but she lifted her hand from Gunnar's head to wrap that arm around Rolf's neck.

"Once we get our cocks in you, mate, fill you with our seed, the claiming will be complete."

Sophia tore her lips from mine and begged, "Please."

"We will give you what you want," Gunnar said, standing to his full height, his hand still buried in her pussy. He lifted her slightly with the strength of his palm pressed to her clit. She whimpered and moved her hips, trying to fuck his hand.

Gods, she was so fucking hot, I had to step back before I spilled my seed like an untried youth.

I glanced at Rolf over her shoulder. I could tell by the way his eyebrow was raised that he, too, had made note of the strength of her reaction. We'd only given her a hint of our seed. What would happen when we stuffed her with three cocks and filled her all at once?

Gunnar withdrew as well, and our mate slumped against Rolf. Panting. Flushed. Her hands spread to the sides slightly behind her as she clung to Rolf for balance. The black cloth covered her eyes and she waited, every curve on display, the rise and fall of her breasts hypnotically beautiful. I could have stared at her for hours.

"What now?" she asked. She licked her lips and whimpered when Rolf pulled his hands away and walked around her to join us. Her back was to the railing.

I stepped back so we could all just look at her, so aroused and needy, desperate.

"Now we fuck you," Gunnar murmured.

I scooped her up in my arms and carried her to the big bed, settled her in the middle. We didn't delay, stripped with a haste brought on only by the need of our mate.

"My cock first, my love," Rolf said, moving over her.

She eagerly parted her thighs for him, cried out when he lowered his chest against hers, cupped her head in his hands. He kissed her, swallowing her cry when he slid into her. Sophia arched her back and lifted her knees to his hips as he began to thrust, in and out.

She tore her mouth from his, angled her head to the side, tilted it back as she cried out, "Oh God. I need... please, oh, harder."

Gunnar and I stood to the sides of the bed and stroked our cocks, watching. It was hard to be patient while Rolf claimed her. While I wasn't jealous of him with Sophia, fucking her and filling her with his seed, I was frustrated that he was deep inside her and not me.

Rolf did as Sophia bid and took her harder, cupping one hand behind her knee and raising it so he could go even deeper. The wet sound of slaps of their fucking filled the room.

"Come, Sophia," Gunnar ordered.

While she hadn't been trained yet to wait for his command to come, Sophia did as he bid. Her body bowed as she cried out her release.

"She's milking my cock. Shit," Rolf groaned. He stiffened above her, plunged deep one last time and came. When his seed filled her, Sophia screamed. Not in pain, but in an orgasmic bliss I was sure she'd never, ever felt before. We'd make her climax with our mouths, our fingers, toys, and we'd watch her as she did it herself. She would feel the instant sizzle of the bliss of it, but it would be nothing like the release when our seed filled her. The power of it was so strong that she would come again, just from it coating her inside and out.

And from three of us, she'd be all but drugged from it. At least at first. And who would resent that? It would taper, the intensity of it, but her need for us—just as we had for her—would never diminish. Our honeymoon period would mean constant fucking. It would mean we'd be insatiable for her and her for us in return. It would mean she would be constantly filled with our seed, all but ensuring it would take root and make a child.

There was no question she would be pregnant by the morning. The idea of her swelling and growing with our child had me ready to come, but I squeezed the base of my cock to stave it off. I wanted to be deep inside her when I did.

Rolf kissed her, gently, deeply, until she slumped, sated, on the bed.

"Rolf," she sighed, catching her breath. Carefully, he pulled from her and sat back on his heels, just staring at her swollen and pink pussy, his seed slipping from her delicate folds. He was still hard and I knew he'd take her again if I didn't practically push him out of the way.

As I knelt on the bed, I pulled her up and into my arms, her knees coming to straddle my thighs. She sat in my lap, my hard cock between us. Fluid seeped from it in a steady stream and I coated her belly with it. I knew the second it began to seep into her, for she came again. It wasn't hard or intense, but a soft, rolling orgasm. I cupped her breasts and gently pinched her nipples as she rode that decadent wave. I pinched harder, testing her and she let her head fall back as she thrust her breasts into my hold. I tugged on them.

"Does that little bit of pain feel good?" I asked.

"Yes!" she cried.

As soon as she answered, I let her nipples go.

"I need to see you. Please, Erik."

I glanced up at Gunnar, not for permission, but in surprise. She knew us, had learned our voices and sensed our differences even after knowing us such a short time.

He, too, seemed surprised, but most likely pleased. Tugging at the knot at the back of the material, it slipped from her eyes and onto the bed.

She blinked those soft brown eyes at me, so sated and relaxed, then smiled.

I couldn't help but stroke over her cheek. So silky soft.

"I've never been like this before," she admitted.

"What? With three men?" I frowned. "I hope not."

She shook her head, her long hair a wild tangle over her shoulders.

"Come like this. I mean, I have. I'm not a virgin or anything." She bit her lip, then glanced at me, then up at Gunnar. Rolf had settled at the head of the bed, his back propped up, contentedly watching. While he'd just fucked her and come—the bastard—he was lazily stroking his hard cock again.

"I'm sorry," she replied. "I shouldn't talk about other men when we're...you know."

Gunnar shook his head. "We need to know all your thoughts, Sophia. Everything about your body. No secrets. Since your orgasms belong to us now, we will know the truth." He narrowed his eyes. "Then we will not speak of it again."

"I've... I've never come with a man before."

At her admission, Rolf's chest all but swelled with egotistical pride.

"And you just came from only my seed touching your skin, my fingers playing with your nipples," I added.

She blushed and bit her lip. "I know. I...I don't understand."

"It's our connection, but also the seed power. With mates, it makes for a powerful connection. Desire will be strong, it will make you needy for more, for our cocks."

"So you're drugging me?" she asked.

I reached between us, coated my fingers, then lifted them to her mouth, slipped them in. She sucked on them, and knew she tasted the muskiness of her arousal mixed with the salty tang of Rolf's seed. Her eyes fell closed and I could feel her body warm all over. When I slipped my fingers free, she licked her lips.

I shrugged in response to her question, grabbed her by the hips and lifted her up and over my cock. Slowly, but with her own weight helping, she impaled herself on me.

Her eyes flared wide. "Does it matter?" I asked. "It feels so fucking good. *You* feel so fucking good." I gripped her ass and shifted her, remaining deep inside her as my cock brushed over new places inside her.

"I'm not going to last, Sophia. You turn us into randy youths."

"I know," Rolf said. "I'm ready for her again."

"Wait your turn," Gunnar growled.

Even through her lust-filled brain, Sophia laughed. "So you're just as drugged with need as I am."

I grunted, lifting her hips and then lowering her back onto me.

"Ride me, Sophia. Show us what feels good." She looked at me with those eyes—fuck, those eyes—then started to move, lifting and lowering. Just watching her breasts sway and bob as she did so had my cock hardening impossibly fuller. Her arousal and Rolf's seed slipped from her, coated my thighs. The thick and heady scent of fucking filled the air.

Her eyes fell closed as she moved, placing her hands on my shoulder for balance as she moved up and down.

"Look at me," I said. Sweat slipped down my brow, slicked the skin between us.

Her eyes fluttered open.

"I want to see you when you come. Don't look away."

Her motions had been tentative to start, eager after that, then quickly became wild with abandon. I took hold of her already hard little nipples and tugged once again, pinched the tender flesh and watched her eyes narrow, saw the surprise there.

"Come all over my cock, Sophia. Milk the seed from me. Take it."

Her eyes flared as I pinched just the slightest bit harder and she came. All the while her inner walls clenched and squeezed my cock, she kept her eyes on me. Her breathy little pants finished me off, my balls tightening, then shooting forth all the seed I'd been saving just for her. Thick and hot, it spurted into her, filling her and marking her as mine.

Our breathing was ragged as we came down from the

delicious release. She was quickly learning that she would not get a tame little orgasm from her men. We would wring every bit of pleasure from her body. And we weren't done.

Gunnar was next.

———

SOPHIA

NO WONDER LEAH WAS HAPPY. THESE VIKEN WARRIORS, were going to fuck me to death. The last orgasm Erik gave me had me practically blacking out. I didn't care if it was the weird seed power that was doing it or if it was their magic cocks. I wanted more. With a loud hiss, Erik lifted me off his cock. A trickle of seed slipped down my legs. I fell back on the bed beside Rolf's legs, sated and smiling. Every single nerve ending in my body was tingling. My pussy was sore yet eager for more.

Gunnar, with his intense dark gaze, watched me as I recovered. His hand slid up and down his impressive shaft. It was long and thick, a dark ruddy red with a large head. Perhaps he was building up the anticipation, perhaps it was him giving me a moment to catch my breath, but when he was finally ready, he reached out, grabbed my ankle and rolled me onto my stomach.

I felt his knee press down on the bed as he hooked an arm about my waist and pulled my hips back so I was butt up, head down.

"Oh, God," I whispered into the blanket.

"Are you ready for more, Sophia?" he asked. I turned my head to look up at him.

He could just take me and he knew I was eager, but he didn't. He wouldn't. He was asking permission. For what, I had no idea. Perhaps he wasn't going to tell me. But I knew that he wouldn't hurt me. He'd showed me that by the way he'd protected me in the forest. He'd showed me time and again by his ridiculous well of patience. He showed me by checking in with me, confirming I wanted him. Wanted what he was going to do.

I didn't want to ask. I didn't need to, because I was going to love it no matter how carnal or dirty or decadent or sweet or wild it was.

I nodded, but remembered he wanted me to say it. "Yes. I'm ready."

He moved behind me so I couldn't see him, but felt his hand stroke up the back of my thigh.

"Good girl."

I shivered at the light touch, but when his fingers stroked over my dripping folds, I almost burst into flames. "We've been gentle with you," he said.

They had? While they hadn't been rough, I wouldn't call what Rolf and Erik had done tame either. They weren't fumbling in the dark. They'd been skilled and talented with their touch—I wouldn't take time to imagine how they'd gained those abilities.

"We might take you one at a time, like we are now, but you have enough holes to please all of us. At the same time."

Gunnar coated his fingers, then moved them to my most forbidden place. I tensed.

"No, I've never—"

His touch was light and gentle, just a touch, nothing more.

"Do you trust me?" he asked.

"I don't... I don't even know you," I replied, thinking solely of his finger on my bottom hole.

"You *know* us, Sophia. Deep down, when you're not thinking about it, your body, even parts of your mind, know that we would never hurt you, that you are our matched mate."

When he began to move in slow circles there, I clenched the blanket, glanced up at Rolf. He nodded once, stroked his finger down my cheek, then slipped it into my mouth.

Rolf bent down so I could stare into his eyes as he fucked my mouth with his finger. "I will take you here while Erik takes your ass. With Gunnar deep in your pussy, you will love it. Just as you're sucking on my finger, so will you take my cock."

Gunnar slid one finger into my ass as Rolf spoke and Erik walked to the opposite side of the bed and reached under my body to stroke my breasts as Gunnar's finger moved in and out of my ass. He coated his finger with something slick and warm, opening me in a way I'd never experienced before.

"Up, Sophia. Up on your hands and knees. Now."

I pushed up as Gunnar instructed Rolf to kiss me and Erik to slide under my chest and suck my nipple into his mouth and touch my clit from beneath.

My left nipple was in Erik's mouth, my right in Rolf's rough hand as he kissed me. Erik's thick fingers spread my pussy lips open, rubbing my clit and I moaned as Gunnar lined his cock up with my pussy, keeping his finger pressed against my back entrance. He slid inside with his cock just as he slid his finger back into my ass. With Rolf's tongue holding me open for his kiss, I had something moving in and out, fucking me, filling me in all three of my holes.

Gunnar began to move deep inside me, stretching me even wider than the other two had, perhaps because he had a finger in my bottom.

"Rolf and Erik might be nice, but I am not." He spat out the word *nice* as if it were tainted. "They might have made you come, taken an orgasm from you, but I will take more."

He stopped talking then, fucking me in earnest. I didn't even mind the feel of his finger sliding in and out along with his cock. I had no idea that there was so much intensity in ass play, that there were so many nerve endings that had come to life.

It was unbelievable. Another layer of pleasure on top of the ones they'd already shown me.

I turned my head away from Rolf's kiss and cried out as my body burned to a cinder surrounded by my mates.

Gunnar hadn't come because he was still fucking me with long, deep strokes. But perhaps his cock was leaking, dripping some of his seed inside me in his eagerness. Whatever the cause, the heat in my body intensified yet again, my heart beating faster than a hummingbird's wing beneath my ribs. My pussy was so swollen, so sensitive that the glide of his cock made me tremble.

"The seed power will always be this potent, Sophia. Give yourself to me. I want to feel you come all over my cock." He thrust faster with his words, driving his thick cock until the tip hit my womb. The finger he had in my ass pressed deeper as well, pulling slightly up, stretching both my pussy and my ass around his possession as Erik's mouth clamped down on my nipple, his fingers rubbing my clit like a high-speed vibrator.

Head thrown back, I cried out, terrified of the tidal wave of sensation flooding me. I tried to control it, to hold back, but Rolf's hand landed in my hair and he angled my head up, forcing me to look into his eyes.

"Gunnar told you to come, mate."

"It's too much."

Rolf held my gaze as his hand landed in a firm strike on my ass. I jolted forward, away from the pain, but the action pushed my clit onto Erik's hand, and had my inner muscles clamping down ever harder on Gunnar's cock and finger.

Behind me, Gunnar groaned. "Spank her again, Rolf. She loves it. Her pussy is like a clamp around my cock."

"Too much!" I cried, frustrated and needy. Tears streamed down my face.

Gunnar spanked me then, the loud crack of it loud. I tensed, then shuddered as I clenched down on his cock and finger. The sharp burn of it had me hissing, but it slowly morphed into heat. Heat that overtook me.

"Give him everything, love," Rolf insisted.

I didn't know what he meant, but then, with instant clarity, I did. I stopped moving, let go of the blanket and exhaled. I relaxed every tense muscle and focused on the feel of Gunnar's cock, of his finger. The first flutter of an orgasm rose within me, but the sharp sting of Gunnar's hand on my ass stopped my release and I cried out, this time in protest.

"Yes, that's it. You'll take what we give you. And what is that?" Rolf asked.

"Pleasure."

"Yes, but when?"

"When you say."

The need coalesced into a brilliant white ball, brighter and brighter as Gunnar fucked me, giving me what I needed. Erik's hand on my clit was an instrument of sensual torture as be stroked me to the edge of release, then stopped. Over and over again.

Gunnar's cock swelled inside me, and I felt a second finger sliding into my bottom, heard his growl as he pressed even deeper. Every bit of my mind was focused on my body, on sensation.

I couldn't breathe, couldn't see, couldn't feel anything but them, the sounds they made, the way they touched me.

"Now, Sophia," Gunnar ordered.

At his command, I came, the ball bursting open, blinding me to anything but sheer bliss. Gunnar's fingers gripped my hips again as he slammed into me and gave me everything. His seed filled me, coated me, marked me permanently and irrevocably as his. I milked his cock and clenched his finger, pulling both into me, wanting to keep them there, to keep the feelings going forever.

I was surrounded by my mates, protected, touched.

Yes, this was what it felt like finally to belong to someone, to give myself completely. Those were my last thoughts when my whole world went dark.

7

"THE THREE OF YOU ARE VERY GOOD AT DISTRACTION," I said, settling my head back against Rolf's chest. We were in the bath, although it was large enough to be like a small pool. The water came up to my neck where I sat in front of my mate, the scented steam swirled and spiraled off the surface. After the sex...God, was that the word for what the four of us had done? The fucking? The...orgy? Well, after all the orgasms they gave me, I'd pretty much blacked out and slept through the night, waking up tucked against Rolf's side. Erik and Gunnar weren't in bed and he'd all but dragged me right to the bath to help ease all my aches.

Yes, taking three men in a row had made me a tad bit sore. And sensitive. And needy all over again.

Rolf shifted against my back, lifting a leg so I was

nestled between his thighs. I could feel his hard cock at my back, but now was not the time even to think of it. I wanted answers, not hot sex. Well, I did want hot sex, but it would have to wait. I could at least control myself for ten minutes in the bath, couldn't I?

The three of them had turned me into a ménage-loving nympho who'd never had bath sex before. I could just lift up and lower myself down and fuck him. What was it called, reverse cowgirl or something?

I realized that Rolf hadn't said anything.

Moving away from him, I spun around, faced him. I'd made little waves that sloshed over the side in my haste. Narrowing my eyes, I stared at the gentlest of the trio. His sly grin said it all. "It's that damn seed power, isn't it?"

He shrugged one broad shoulder. "I can't help that I desire you, that my pre-cum seeps from my cock nonstop with you around."

I pursed my lips, for I couldn't be angry. Not when just his cock rubbing against my bottom made me feel so good. Having all three of them come deep inside me had ensured I would always be eager for them. I *should* hate the idea, but I couldn't. I wasn't a drugged sex slave. I was their match, their mate and I wanted them. It. Sex.

Fucking.

"Distraction," I repeated. "Let's talk bad guys."

"Bad guys?"

I leaned back against the opposite end of the tub, settled in. I wanted answers and I knew if I got out, I wouldn't get them. I'd get something else entirely.

"The VSS."

All playfulness slipped from his face.

"I want to know about them."

Rolf sighed, the laughter fading from his eyes, the playfulness gone. He didn't look sad, exactly. More resigned.

"They are the Viken Sector Separatist movement. They are led by a coalition of very powerful families, families that ruled Viken's sectors as three separate countries before the Hive wars reached us."

I nodded. "Just like Earth. We still have a bunch of different governments."

"Exactly. We had three, and they ruled for centuries. But when the Hive wars reached us, they were forced to unite under the strongest ruler."

"Lev, Drogan and Tor? The three Kings?"

"No, love. Their great grandfather. He was the first high King of Viken. But the sector leaders did not want to give up power. They've never accepted the unification."

I rolled my eyes. "Powerful people never want to give up their position. It's the same on Earth. I know all about that." I rubbed some of the sweet-scented soap over my arms and shoulders, thinking. "So, they started a secret organization to overthrow the three Kings?"

"No." Rolf's eyes tracked the movements of my hands as I rubbed soap over my chest and neck, then lower, onto my breasts just beneath the water. He was so focused on my hands he missed my naughty-girl grin entirely. Men. "The VSS formed decades ago. Their efforts culminated in the death of the three Kings' parents when they were infants."

What a political mess. "So, the three Kings were split up when they were babies and sent to each of the sectors to grow up."

"Yes." His gaze lifted to my lips, so I licked them,

enjoying the darkening of his pupils and the stutter in his speech. "The King and Queen were dead. I was just a boy, not much older than the three Kings. They were sent to grow up with guardians in each of the sectors, to learn their ways and customs, to be an accepted part of the community, a champion of their people."

I lowered my head into the water and rinsed my hair. Rising, I lifted my head and studied the various bottles that lined the tub. Which one was the shampoo? They should have labels or something. "And did it work?" I picked up a cream-colored glass bottle, removed the stopper and lifted it to my nose.

Eww. No. That was totally man scent.

I scrunched my nose and placed it back on the ledge. A red bottle. Looked promising. I wrapped my fingers around it, but Rolf's hand closed around mine.

"What are you looking for, mate?"

"Shampoo." I lifted the stopper to my nose. Interesting. More like sandalwood. I wanted something sweet.

Rolf pulled me closer and reached for a white bottle the looked like smoked glass. "Allow me."

He poured a bit of pale green liquid into his palm and I was worried I would smell like seaweed or pine trees, but the scent was light and sweet, like a glass of summer lemonade with extra sugar.

With a sigh, I relaxed into his care and moaned as he massaged my scalp with tender fingers.

I'd never had a man wash my hair. Talk about addictive. "God, you can do that every day."

"It will be my pleasure, Sophia." His voice was deep, rich, and all traces of jesting were gone.

Distraction. Distraction. Distraction.

What the hell had we been talking about?

"So, did it work? Did they grow up loyal to their sectors or whatever? Wouldn't that cause a problem when they had to get back together?"

Rolf chuckled and lowered his hands to massage my shoulders. "Yes, it worked. Too well. The brothers refused to reunite. Their allegiances and prejudices firmly in place, as the VSS wanted."

"So what happened? They get along fine now." I'd meet Lev several times, but knew from my conversations with Leah that her men were a united force, just as mine appeared to be.

"Leah happened. She united the three Kings, just as you have united Gunnar, Erik and me"

"You're each from a different sector?"

"Yes."

"Oh." Understanding dawned. Leah, Earth girl Leah, had united an entire planet by forcing her mates to learn how to get along. And then... "Allayna. The baby."

"The one true Queen of Viken." Rolf dipped my head gently, rinsing the soap from the long strands with slow, relaxing strokes.

I closed my eyes and pictured that cute little pixie with her red hair and bright blue eyes. "She's not even one yet."

"She is the future of our planet. The three Kings grew up in the sectors. And, as the Kings are loyal to their people, the sectors are loyal to them. Allayna is their daughter, the one all the sectors recognize as the true heir. They might refuse one of the three Kings, but none would refuse her. She is adored and revered in every sector."

"So, they have to kill her."

"We believe that is their goal, yes."

"So they intended to transport Leah and her baby to the wilds instead of me?"

Rolf nodded. "Yes."

"But how did it work, how did I get sent there instead?"

"We're not sure. A transport glitch. The Kings have entire teams of engineers working on answering that very question."

I opened my eyes and looked up into his face, meeting his gaze. "I'm not thrilled about someone trying to kill me, but I'm glad it happened."

Rolf's jaw clenched. "Glad?"

"If their transport plans had worked, Leah would have died protecting her baby. I...I can't think about how awful that would have been."

Rolf just made a weird guttural sound as a reply and released me. I righted myself and ran my hands over my hair to get the excess water out.

"So Gunnar and I will go to this place...Club Trinity, and find the man who wanted to kill Leah."

Rolf reached for a washcloth and I stared at the way the water sluiced off his broad shoulders and down over his flat nipples. "No, love. Erik is meeting with the Kings. Gunnar's already gone."

"Gone?"

Nodding, he picked up the soap I'd been using and rubbed it over the washcloth. I breathed in the scent of vanilla. Did they have vanilla on Viken?

"Give me your arm."

I lifted it in the air and he took my hand as he ran the bubbly washcloth up and down. If he wanted to do this as he gave me answers, I wasn't going to complain. I'd never been washed by anyone before, at least not since I was a baby, and it was pretty darn nice.

"You're doing this to distract me," I fake grumbled.

Rolf switched arms.

"I can do both. Clean you, so Erik and I can make you dirty again, and give you the answers to your questions."

That, I could live with.

"Gunnar went to Central City to see if he can learn more about the man with the mark."

"The bad guy."

Rolf frowned. "Yes, him. Gunnar plans to go to Club Trinity and reestablish his connections. He hasn't been in some time."

"He went without me? I want to help!"

He cocked a brow. "And how would you help at a sex club, mate?"

"I'm the only one who knows what the man sounds like. I can identify him."

Rolf gave me a dark look. I assumed it wasn't directed at me, but at the man who I could recognize by voice.

"I told you, I know about power struggles. I got caught up in the mafia on Earth. I want to help. Need to," I added. "I tried to play nice last time, and all that got me a prison sentence."

"And us," Rolf added, absently washing my shoulders.

"And you. But I can't let this one go, Rolf. They were going to kill Leah and the baby. They tried to kill me!" I cried, my heart rate accelerating with frustration and anger. "I'm the only one who can identify him. I have to go. We can't stand by and do nothing. They'll try again. As long as Allayna is alive, they'll keep trying."

"Don't remind me," Rolf grumbled.

"Let me help," I repeated.

"We spoke of this while you were sleeping, before Gunnar left. He has to investigate alone. If he showed up at the club with you on his arm, there would be questions. It would be obvious you were the mate that transported yesterday."

"The bad guy didn't know I saw his tattoo," I countered. "And, he thinks I'm dead. Perhaps Gunnar is a newly mated Viken who just wants to show me his lifestyle."

He glanced up at me. "True, but when he, the bad guy, discovers you're not dead in the wilds, he'll try again. You're a liability to him."

"A loose end," I added.

He furrowed his brow. "Like a thread?"

I smiled. "An Earth expression. In this case, I am someone who knows what he's done, how he wanted the Queen and her baby. Like you said, a liability. They'll try to take me out."

"Take you out? To where?"

I laughed. As well as these NPU translators worked, some things just didn't translate well. "They'll try to kill me."

"Stand."

I looked at him for a moment as he added more soap to the washcloth.

I did as he wanted and water sluiced down my body.

From his position, Rolf was at eye level with my pussy, and he stared at it avidly. He even licked his lips.

He cleared his throat and knelt before me, ran the washcloth over my belly. "Gunnar will not place you in danger unless there is no other choice, unless he can't learn the truth on his own. I understand your history now and your...eagerness to find the Viken traitor, but Gunnar must work alone first. He is going to cross-reference the Central City transport logs with known masters at the club . You know the bad guy transported from the wilds somewhere. There is a record of it and Gunnar will find it."

That made sense.

"What if he can't?" I asked. "I'm not doubting Gunnar, but bad guys are slippery. They cover their tracks. What if he can't learn the truth?"

"Then you will have to be undercover."

"Undercover?"

The washcloth moved up and over my breasts, cleaning them with much more attention than they probably needed.

"A training submissive. Gunnar will have to take you into the club . Unfortunately, he is quite well-known there. He will have to perform a scene with you."

My eyes fell closed as Rolf plucked my nipple through the washcloth.

"A scene? What kind of scene?"

I heard the wet slap of the washcloth against the edge of the tub.

"Bondage, service sex such as sucking Gunnar's cock, punishment, anal. There are many possibilities."

"But I've never done those kinds of things," I

countered, blinking down at my mate. Both hands now cupped my breasts, played and tugged at my nipples. I gasped at one sharp pinch.

Rolf stared up at me, and the look in his eyes made me nervous. "If you prefer, Gunnar can do a scene with another woman in the club. Sometimes, the submissive is forced to watch, and not participate."

"So, I would have to sit there and watch Gunnar have sex with someone else?"

Rolf dropped his eyes to my thighs as the scene floated in my mind. Gunnar with another woman's mouth on his cock, taking his seed. Gunnar thrusting into another woman's body as I knelt on the floor, helpless and silent, watching my mate fuck another woman. "No. I don't want him touching anyone else."

Rolf grinned up at me, but it was not a happy grin. "Gunnar will be pleased. We discussed this at length before he left. He believes you would be unaffected."

"Does he want another woman?" The thought made my heart hurt, and I'd only known him for one damn day.

"No, love." Rolf lifted a finger to my lips to silence my protest. "It was agreed, Erik and I will prepare you, get you ready for the club."

"Prepare me?"

Rolf moved closer to me, slid his hands down my belly, over my hips to cup my pussy.

"First, we will shave you here. I like this little bit of fluff you have—"

"It's called a landing strip."

He looked up at me with a quirked brow. "For a fighting ship?"

I bit my lip. I'd never really thought about the name

for the waxing style. "I guess so. I think it's to make sure a man knows where to go."

Rolf laughed then. He was so quick to do so and I enjoyed that about him. But that didn't mean he was any less virile or insistent.

"It has to go. You will need to have a smooth and bare pussy for Trinity."

Huh. Okay, I guess that was fine.

He cupped me again.

"Instead of telling you, why don't we show you?"

I smiled at the way he was looking up at me, all wicked boy.

"Good idea."

"Erik!" Rolf called. He cupped my pussy, slipped his finger through my folds and then into me. I gripped his shoulder so I didn't fall over.

My other mate came into the bathroom.

"Is she clean?" he asked.

"Not for long," Rolf countered. "She is ready."

Erik grunted, then came over and held out a hand. "Come, love. Let's get that pretty pussy all shaved, then I'll lick all that newly smooth flesh. We'll see just how sensitive you are."

"She just got wet," Rolf added, taking his finger from me and putting it in his mouth. "And I'm going to lick that pussy, not you," he growled.

No seed power was involved in making me hot and horny this time. Just Rolf's skilled hands.

As I stepped from the tub and Erik dried me off, I said to them, "This shouldn't be too bad."

Little did I know that when Erik was eating me out just a little while later, I would be eating my words.

Rolf

Erik made quick work of inspecting every inch of our mate's body. Her bare skin was smooth as glass and smelled like flowers. Surely it would make everything more sensitive for her, if that were even possible.

Her hair was still wet and slicked back from her face, making her eyes look bigger, her face more delicate. She was truly beautiful, and brave. Perhaps even a little embarrassed having the two of us see her so intimately, yet touch her in a way that was much more clinical than passionate. But that would change. Now.

Erik's dark hair was wet as well, and I knew he'd planned to work out with the new guard recruits early this morning. He must have bathed in the guard quarters.

No matter. Our mate couldn't take her eyes off him as he stripped out of his uniform. Her breasts rose and fell and her long, shapely legs were already spread open in welcome.

I wore nothing more than a towel as I walked to the side of the bed and scooped her into my arms.

"Hey! What are you doing? I thought we were—" Her words faded and her cheeks turned pink with a delicate blush.

"We are, love, just not on the bed."

"Oh." Her eyes widened as I carried her to the swing Gunnar had installed when we'd been asked to take a mate. The swing was designed for a woman's pleasure. Wide straps would support her body and her limbs, holding her in place for our attention, and also restraining her movement.

I settled her back into it, looked into her eyes as I waited for her to settle—mind and body. I held her still as Erik took her left arm, lifted it out to her side strapping her arm and wrist in the thick restraints. He tested the bond, ensured it wasn't too tight.

I didn't mind sharing Sophia with Erik. Or Gunnar. My mother hadn't given her attention or love evenly between my brother and me. I knew how that could hurt, could damage your soul. So I shared my mate with the others easily because I wanted her to have all the love we could give. I wanted her to know all of us, and I knew Erik and Gunnar wouldn't just take and take. They'd give. And at the center? Sophia. Always.

"I don't know about this."

Erik stopped and our mate's gaze darted from Erik to me and back again. His was dark and intense, appropriate for what Sophia would be facing at the club. "This is mild, mate, compared to what you might see in the club. It might seem a little...scary, but remember, we will never hurt you. We will never take you without you wanting it. If you wish to refuse, we will understand. Gunnar doesn't want you anywhere near the place."

Sophia bit her lip and looked up at me. I shrugged. It had to be her decision. "Erik is right, love. If you can't handle this, then you will struggle with whatever Gunnar has planned for you at the club." I stroked her cheek. "And that is fine. We aren't mad. Not in the slightest. We just need to know your boundaries."

"Perhaps it's good that we've discovered this here," Erik countered.

Sophia lifted her free hand.

"No. Do it. Do whatever you have to do. I'm not letting that asshole kill Leah or Allayna."

"Not at the expense of your fear of us. When we fuck, when we play like this, it should be all pleasure."

"It will be," she said.

"Not if you're afraid," Erik added.

Sophia bit her lip. "I'm not afraid. Really. It's all just… daunting. I've loved everything so far that you've done. I'm sure I'll love this."

I glanced at Erik, then to Sophia. "All right. But if you need us to stop, we will. Immediately. Something to remember, love, is that you have all the power. We won't do this to you unless you allow it. You give us your submission, but then we give the power right back."

"I can say stop," she replied, settling back.

"Exactly." Erik nodded and we quickly strapped her into place.

I was pleased she'd taken a moment to understand. It would be better for her now, this knowledge that she was the key to the four of us, the central cog in the wheel. Without her, we were…just mere warriors. And all three of us were ready for more.

As I watched Sophia's mind settle, become aroused by our attentions, my cock was so hard it felt like a lead weight between my legs, painful. Heavy. Her perfect body was laid out before us like a feast—her arms and legs were splayed wide and strapped into the swing. Her pink pussy was open and on display, hanging in the air at the perfect level for me to drop to my knees and feast. And, with her head leaned back, she could take Erik's cock in her mouth as I indulged myself at her core.

Erik met my gaze and I saw an eagerness there I understood all too well. "Shall we begin?"

"Yes." I stepped close to Sophia's pussy as Erik walked to her head. I placed my hand on her stomach and spread my fingers wide, nearly covering her. Her skin was so warm, so silky soft. She shuddered at my touch and I knew she was ready.

Erik stood above her and leaned forward so his cock dangled in front of her lips as his hands rested on her breasts. "Are you ready for the rules, Sophia?"

Her pussy glistened and I ran my fingers along the slick folds, but denied her what she really wanted. No penetration. No rubbing of her clit. She would have to wait until Erik was finished with the rules Gunnar had given us.

"No one exists but us. If you look at anyone else, you'll be spanked."

Sophia blinked up at him in confusion. "But, there's no one here."

I chuckled and reached to the wall closest me. We were in the corner of the room, but as the shutters drifted open on silent gears, the wide-open windows allowed anyone on the upper levels of the fortress to witness our mate's pleasure.

"Oh my God." Sophia jerked her wrists against the restraints. "I didn't know. I..."

She looked at Erik but I answered her. "Shh, they'll see how beautiful you are, how you give us the most incredible pleasure. They will be jealous of us, your mates."

"I am proud of you as our mate and I wish for

everyone to see you. Rolf does too. He finds immense pleasure in sharing you. Not by touch," Erik added.

"Never," I growled. "They can see how gorgeous you are, how perfect you are for us, but nothing more. Ever."

"The rule again. No one exists but us. If you look at anyone else, you'll be spanked."

I watched as she considered our words, the possibility of being seen, before she relaxed into the straps. Gave over.

"Gunnar will be touching you at the club. It will be crowded. Eyes will be on you. Watching you love whatever Gunnar does to you. They'll see you come and be envious of him."

Erik walked around our mate, petting her for everyone watching to see. Sector One's fixation on public displays of ownership, of a mate's ability to bring his female pleasure, were the talk of the other sectors. The only thing Erik might love more than the three warriors staring down at us from across the courtyard on the third level was taking Sophia in the ass, and that was coming. Soon.

"Open up," Erik said, nudging her full lips with the dripping head of his cock. His pre-cum coated her skin and I watched as it seeped in, as she flicked her tongue out to lick it up.

"Oh," she moaned, the seed power settling over her like a warm blanket. It would help her with her nerves, with any apprehension she had. It was all right for her to be nervous, for we would push her boundaries. But fear, no. Never.

Widening her mouth, she took the broad head of Erik's cock and then part of his shaft. Erik's breath hissed out as he put a hand on her cheek, then began to move in and out of her, not very deep to allow her time to adjust. He wasn't small and the angle was surely new for her.

I wasn't going to just stare at them. No. I was going to prepare her to take all of us at the same time, then fuck her.

"So smooth, love," I commented, sliding my finger over the now bare outer lips of her pussy. "Feel that?"

She moaned, for it had to be extra sensitive. Her pussy was gorgeous, so pink and wet and swollen. So eager.

Picking up the small butt plug, I squeezed some lubricant onto the hard object, coating it thoroughly. Then I placed my slick fingers at her back entrance and circled, spreading the slick ointment. Coating her in it.

She bucked at my touch, but couldn't speak, for she had her mouth full. Very full.

"Ever had your ass fucked, love?" I murmured, continuing to circle and press slightly against her tight hole.

Her head shook from side to side ever so slightly.

"We'll take you here, play with you, fill you. You're going to love it. I promise." I looked down between her spread legs, saw wetness slipping from her as I was able to breach the tight ring of muscle and slip just the tip of my finger into her.

"All three of us are going to fuck you at once. Ah, love, you're so good at sucking cock," Erik growled.

"One of us in your mouth, one in your pussy, and another in your ass. Fucking you, filling you. Loving you."

Pulling the finger free, she moaned, but I pressed the plug to her and started working it in. With the lube, it wasn't hard to do, for the plug was small and her eagerness even surprised her. When it settled into place, I watched as her free hand came up and cupped Erik's balls, eager for more. He had moved close enough for her to touch, despite the restraints, and she took advantage.

"Oh, no, love." Erik, while I knew he loved her hand on him—my balls tightened in jealousy—couldn't allow her to have what she wanted in this. Not this time. Oh, we'd give her the chance to take charge, to touch us, play with us, but not now. She needed to learn that we would *give* her her pleasure, the way it was done at Club Trinity.

Erik moved her hand away from him and tightened the strap around her wrist, tested the comfort of it, all the while Sophia eagerly sucked on his cock.

"Fuck," he whispered at her voraciousness.

I couldn't wait any longer. She'd given over so beautifully that I couldn't hold back. Lining my weeping cock up to her entrance, I slid right in.

She moaned as I filled her, the fit so tight with the plug.

Once I settled all the way in, I looked up at Erik. His jaw was clenched, but his hand on her cheek was gentle.

"Ready?" I asked. He nodded once.

"Ready, Sophia?"

She tugged at the bonds on her hands, but moaned and settled.

Erik and I moved our hands to the straps on the swing, gripped them, then began to rock the swing ever so gently.

She was pinned between us, being fucked in her mouth and pussy. None of us moved, the swing doing all the work. We gauged the motions based on watching

Sophia. We couldn't allow the swing to move too far, for we didn't know how far she could take a cock into her mouth, her throat.

But she was surprising us, taking a little bit more, then more still as time went on.

She came, milking my cock as we continued the pace, never stopping. First one orgasm, then another.

"See, Sophia, only pleasure. Anyone seeing you will know we are giving you just what you need. And in just a second, they'll see us take it from you."

"Fuck, yes. I can't take her sweet suction any longer. I'm going to come, love. Swallow."

When Erik groaned and I watched Sophia's throat work to swallow all the seed he was giving her, I couldn't hold back any longer. The pleasure of her hot pussy, the tightness of it, the way she responded to both Erick and me, had my orgasm build at the base of my spine, draw my balls up and shoot forth, filling her, coating, marking her.

She moaned around Erik's cock, but he pulled out as soon as he was done and she screamed. Her inner walls clenched and milked my cock, ensuring every last drop was pulled from me. There was nothing left. She'd claimed me just as much as I had her.

"Beautiful, love."

Once she settled, her breathing becoming more even, we undid the straps and lifted her from the swing. Erik closed the blind on the window, blocking out the rest of the world once again.

As I carried her across the room to the bed, she glanced back at it. "That was...wow. If that's what it's going to be like at the club , then I'm ready. I want more."

She nuzzled into me and I realized we had awakened something inside her that she hadn't even known about. There was no going back now. Not that any of us wanted to. But I had no doubt that what was to come might rip us all apart. The VSS was just too big for the four of us alone.

unnar

I RUBBED MY HAND OVER MY FACE, TRIED TO WIPE AWAY THE gritty feeling in my eyes. My day in Central City had been a waste. Well, not completely. I'd discovered that the transport data for the shitty little station in the wilds had been wiped clean. Not only was there no record of any Vikens transporting in and out earlier in the day, there was no record of our transport to find Sophia, nor the one of the King and Queen that followed. Nor our return to the City. How the fuck did transports of over ten people just get erased?

On purpose. So while I hadn't found the bastard, his actions to cover his identity were not subtle and easily proved his guilt, if only we knew who he was. The VSS wanted the Queen and the baby. Wanted them dead. I wasn't sure if I should be thankful their plan had been foiled or not. The thought of Sophia fending off her attacker, shooting him with the Viken's own ion pistol when she could have been easily killed instead, made me want to punch a hole in the wall. But if the transport error hadn't occurred, the planet would be in crisis. The Queen and princess would surely be dead.

With the Kings aware of the danger to their mate and child, every precaution was put in place. Neither would be left alone and, fortunately, three Viken warrior husbands would watch over them. Transports for the two of them would be only in an emergency and they would transport with at least one of the Kings. Guards were doubled.

While investigators were put on to the case, the only true lead, the only witness to the crime was Sophia. And it all came down to the fucking mark she'd seen on the fucker's forearm. Only the true Masters would have the mark. That meant the group of possibilities was small, considering the lead, but too many to be able to identify someone immediately. And so my plan to keep Sophia from being involved in finding the traitor was not going to happen. We—the entire planet—needed her.

Fuck, I needed her, and not just to find the bastard. My cock ached for her. Being so far away, my being in Central City while she was safe on Viken United with Rolf and Erik, was almost painful. I was sure they were taking good care of her, that she was safe, ensuring that her craving for cock was filled. The seed power had been impressively strong, but our mate was a passionate woman and I had to think she would still have craved our attentions—from all three of us—without it.

Her craving was my withdrawal and I was eager to have her beneath me again. Just... with me. She was able to break through a wall I'd put around my heart, a little at a time. What I'd shared with Loren had been... love, but this, what I had with Sophia was something else entirely. It had to be the match, for we were so perfect a fit. It hurt, the knowledge that I could lose her. But I wanted her more.

And so it was with mixed feelings that I used my InterCom and connected with the others. I wanted to hear her voice, to know that she was safe, but did not wish to tell her of my findings. I wanted to shield her from anything bad. She would need to help, and be put in danger.

After sharing my findings, Sophia spoke. I got hard at just the soft sound.

"I'm ready, Gunnar. Take me to the club. I'm the only one who can identify him."

I knew the latter, so I disregarded it. "You're ready?" I asked. It was more than just being prepared to track down a killer, but for a night at the club.

"Yes. Erik and Rolf have...oh God, I can't say it over the phone. Or whatever this communication thing is."

I had no idea what a phone was, but I assumed it was an Earth contraption.

"Sophia." I deepened my voice to the tone I'd use on her when we were in the club. "If you are going to go to Club Trinity with me, saying what your mates did to prepare you should not embarrass you. Trust me, I will push you farther than you can ever imagine."

She was quiet for a moment and I heard a little

breathy sigh. "Yes, you're right. They shaved me, put me in a swing and they...they fucked my mouth and pussy."

I almost came in my pants, thinking of her spread between them, taking them both. Of how they had pushed her.

"What else?" I asked.

"And a plug."

I couldn't help it, I had to adjust myself, my pants now much too tight.

"I'm ready," she repeated.

So was I.

"Transport here," I said, my words rough with need and eagerness. Yes, then I could touch her, feel her, know she was real and safe and mine. "I will meet you at the transport station."

"I do not wish to transport alone," Sophia replied. I could hear the thread of fear in her voice. I could only imagine she was afraid of traveling unaccompanied. Her first experience with this kind of travel had led to near disaster.

"Do not worry," Rolf murmured. "We will be with you."

"That's right, love. There's no fucking way you'll do that again by yourself. Not for a long time," I all but growled, thinking of how close we had been to losing her. Even before we ever had her.

"Not until the VSS is wiped out," Erik added. "We need an hour."

"I'll meet you then. Don't be late." I didn't want to take Sophia into the club, but my duty was to protect the royal family. And Sophia. If, no, when the man who'd ordered her death discovered she was alive, he'd come after her, too. Therefore, I'd protect her with my life, all the while finding the bastard and saving the royal females. "Be prepared, Sophia. Tonight we go to Club Trinity."

———

GUNNAR, CENTRAL CITY, OUTSIDE OF CLUB TRINITY

I ESCORTED SOPHIA INTO THE HEART OF THE entertainment district. We walked down the glittering walkway less than a block from the inconspicuous entrance to Club Trinity, my hand on her back. There were no trees here, no wilds. This was the most urban place on the planet. Central City was a megacity on the northern continent of Viken. Also called simply "Central" or "The City", it was the one place on Viken where our people embraced the most advanced technologies that Viken's membership in the Interstellar Coalition had afforded. Transport stations, food synthesizers, advanced communications and simulator systems, entertainment and music, food and drink from all over the galaxy could be found in the city.

The city served as Viken's main trade port with the other member planets. As a result, the city was vibrant and full of life. Any appetite could be sated here, good or bad. The dark underbelly of the sparkling lights and fast-paced lifestyle had once held singular appeal for me. As a young man trying to bury the pain of my past, I'd drowned my grief here, in sex, drink, power and the pursuit of every pleasure.

Now, returning here with Sophia by my side made me

physically ill. I did not want her here, where the scum of the planet sat at the table next to sector leaders and council members, selling secrets and loyalty as easily as a piece of ripe fruit at market.

I'd been around the noble warriors of the Coalition Fleet for long years, fought alongside the most noble soldiers from every world. Upon my return to Viken, I'd served only the three Kings and their new mate. All honorable men. All worthy of my respect.

Coming back to Central City felt like a betrayal of everything I fought to protect.

But I was a realist. I knew how things worked. The city was as necessary to Viken's survival as the atmosphere that protected the planet. And there were honorable people here. They fought and scrambled against the constant tide of greed and corruption that opposed them.

It was a struggle that would never end, and one I tired of. Now that I had a mate, my brothers Rolf and Erik, and a royal family I respected, I had no wish to return to the loneliness of my past. For once, I did not want to be alone. I wanted my mate, my family.

I wanted to track the bastard who'd tried to kill my mate and gut him so I could go home and enjoy Sophia. Protect her. Care for her. Make her fall in love with me. I wanted her to love me. I wanted her to look at me, not with fear or anxiety, but with love. Trust. Longing.

Fuck. I sounded like a woman, but perhaps it was worth it.

I squeezed Sophia's side with that thought and she jumped, her gaze darting quickly to mine, then away.

"I know you told me what to expect, but I'm still nervous."

Sophia was covered completely by a long cloak with a hood. Beneath, she wore nothing. While the dress of females in Central City was different than the long garments of those in the Sectors, neither was appropriate for going to the club.

A submissive or slave at Club Trinity, whether male or female, did not require clothing. "Good."

She glanced up at me, her face not hiding her surprise.

"You should be nervous. If you weren't, people would begin to question," I clarified. "As long as you're not nervous about being with *me,* then everything is fine."

I stopped outside the large door. By looking at it, no one would know what was behind it, the mix of depravity, sensuality and submission that was within. Only a small plaque with the club's mark, placed discretely to the right of the entrance, identified its location.

Leaning down, I murmured in Sophia's ear, "Whatever you see, whatever you feel, remember, I will never leave your side. If you hear the man's voice, you will give me the signal. Nothing more."

We'd decided on a way for her to communicate that she'd heard the Viken responsible for her attempted murder. When she mentioned an interest in having a woman touch her, I would know the bastard was close. It was a complete lie since she had three men to touch and please. If her proclivities leaned toward an encounter with a woman, we would not deny her, but we knew this not to be the case. The matching proved it. And so it was the perfect signal. If she spoke the words, found the man we hunted, I would take care of the rest.

While she nodded, I repeated, "Your only job is to obey me, listen for his voice and signal when you hear it. Your part will be done. Nothing more." I repeated the last, more for my benefit than hers since the four of us had gone over it again and again all day long. Erik and Rolf most likely felt like caged animals waiting for us to return.

Unfortunately, only members were allowed inside the club. Neither Rolf nor Erik would make it past the security check just inside the front door.

"All right," she replied.

I arched a brow. "Have you forgotten so soon?"

She frowned as I waited patiently for her to remember the need for a formal address inside the club. "Yes, Sir."

I gave one quick nod. "Good. From this moment on, you obey. If you don't, the consequences will match the club's protocol." Spanking. Flogging. Humiliation. She was mine, but if she insulted another Master, with or without intending to do so, I would be forced to punish her accordingly.

Tugging on the door, I escorted my mate into my world. My *old* world.

The building was three stories tall. The main floor was meant for members to meet and mingle. With rich banquettes for seating that surrounded a dance floor in a semicircle, it was easy to watch and be watched. It was only when a connection was made that the new lovers might venture to the other floors.

Those from Sector One, where men liked to claim

their mates while others watched, only need escort their lover through a doorway that led to the play area on the other side of the large room. There, floor-to-ceiling glass walls allowed everyone in the main room to see into three sizable playrooms. Within, members did anything they wanted while being watched. If that wasn't enough, the room contained every possible tool or device for making anal play fun and wild.

I took a breath, imagined my mate bent over one of those benches as I inserted a plug in her ass and fucked her into submission.

As we entered the black-walled foyer to the club, the three-headed serpent, the same symbol burned into my flesh, rose as tall as I, the dark red outline shining like fresh blood on the floor as we approached the security checkpoint. The giant Viken warrior guarding the inner door was not one I recognized.

He looked at Sophia, his eyes lingered on my mate's perfect pink lips until I stepped forward, breaking his eye contact with my beautiful mate.

The guard just grunted and grinned at me, without apology.

That was Club Trinity, every carnal desire not just openly shared, but embraced.

"She's beautiful," the guard said.

"I know. And she's mine. I don't share."

The guard shrugged. "Let me know if you change your mind, or tire of her attentions." He held out a small scanning device and I lifted my wrist to expose the mark there. Beneath the mark was a small chip embedded in my flesh, marking me as a member of the club, as one of the elite.

Sophia and I were checked for weapons by two other guards before the man with the scanner cleared us to enter the club. "Welcome back, Master Gunnar. It's been a long time."

"Thank you." A long time? Twelve years. It felt like a lifetime ago.

With my hand around Sophia's waist, I led her into the main ballroom. Dozens of unmated men and women mingled, looking for partners, for sex, for pain. Any appetite was welcome here.

The low light level in the main room ensured the level-one rooms were on prominent display. On the other side of the glass, brightly lit participants carried out every sex act I could think of.

I could only imagine Sophia's thoughts when the first sex scenes she witnessed were public fucking, exhibitionism and anal play.

She leaned into me, her small hand searching for mine and I gently entwined my fingers with hers. Squeezed. I had warned her, had, in fact, described the club , and its three levels in great detail.

The second floor catered toward the likes of those from Sector Three. It was one large room, bacchanal style, for anyone to touch or suck or lick, kiss or fuck any other. It was decadent and occupied with those who wanted to focus on oral pleasure, with anyone and everyone within reach. Sector Three was known for their love of oral sex, their tongues quite skilled, and anyone seeking that kind of pleasure knew to seek someone from that region of Viken, and on the second floor.

The third floor was where I felt most comfortable. It was the darker floor, with soft lighting, dark red leather everywhere. It had restraints and toys, whatever anyone needed to dish out pain along with their pleasure. Level three was about control. But that was for later.

We circled the lower two levels for over an hour, my mate walking discreetly behind me, never more than a single step from my side. I'd forgotten the intensity of the carnal temptations offered by this place. Everywhere I looked, men and women played and screamed, fucked and bled. I was not into true pain, I was not a Sadist, but I did not judge their need. Nor the needs of the submissives quivering with desire as their asses were struck by the crop or cane.

But I could not deny the seductive nature of the club's atmosphere, my cock hard and ready the entire length of our tour. The place was created for fucking and the air exuded an essence of need. Harnessed power. Desire. I felt it and I knew Sophia had too. But we both had to wait.

I knew she focused on listening to the voices of those around us, particularly the Masters marked with the Trinity Serpent, as I was. I took her to every dark corner, every lounge and bar. And she listened, she followed behind me like a shadow. Once or twice, when we passed a woman being fucked or spanked, usually both, her gentle hands would settle at the small of my back. Even through the black leather I wore, I could feel her trembling. But with desire or fear, I could not say.

Not yet. When I knew we were safe, knew the bastard who'd tried to kill her was not here, only then would I look into her eyes and see the truth. If her gaze held fear, I would take her from this place and whisk her away to the safety of our private quarters in the city where Erik, Rolf and I would see to her needs. Strangely, this place held no pull for me when judged against my mate's desires. She came first. There had been a time when this club had been a second home to me, a place I belonged. A place where I would not be judged but accepted for who and what I was.

A demanding Dominant that sought control. I needed it almost on a cellular level. A warrior's life was not guaranteed to be long. Fighting the Hive, many Vikens didn't return. Somehow, Erik, Rolf and I had all survived, outlived the horrors that engaging and defending our home planet from the insidious Hive wrought. It never ended. Even with us no longer on the front lines, the war continued.

With our service complete, we'd taken roles as the Kings' guards. While it was less deadly than the front lines, there was still the threat. The VSS. Who needed the Hive when the VSS would destroy our own planet? Life was always tense, constant danger, imminent death. And so the club was an outlet to purge the darkness.

For me, I could wield a crop, a flogger, my hand, or even my cock to give a submissive what they needed. I took control from a lover to ease her burden, to provide a safe haven for her pain or pleasure, her rage or despair. I needed to break my lovers' boundaries, free them from the cage of their own minds.

It was a fine dance, the balance between me and the female I dominated. But that was all it had been, a dance. One carnal song, and then it was over. Without a backward glance, I moved on. I'd soothed the part of me that needed taming, needed control, at least for a prescribed amount of time. When finished, I'd be sated, mentally and physically. Nothing more.

Now, with the little hand warming my lower back, there was more. Too much more. I couldn't dominate and fuck Sophia and walk away. I knew what she wanted, what she needed, how to push her to take even *more*, but I would never allow her to walk away. She was mine.

She would give over all her secrets, yet so would I. And that was the difference. The club was filled with bodies, with people desperate for connection or release, and yet it was so empty of soul, of intimacy. Of love. There was nothing here, no connection deeper than a quick fuck.

The air we breathed was tainted with shallowness. Just having Sophia see this, to know how empty I used to be, had me wanting to whisk her from the building, scrub her clean of the tawdry filth and sink into her. She was good. She was everything I'd never known I was missing.

I didn't need the casual acceptance the club offered. I had found the bonds of brotherhood with Erik and Rolf, and now, with the desire and trust I'd witnessed in Sophia's dark eyes. I just had to hope she didn't think less of me, see me with jaded eyes.

When this hunt was done, I'd look there, in her eyes, and see if they held lust. Desire. Longing. Could she see past the veneer of the club to understand what I'd needed from it? Would she want the same? I had to hope the mating, the match, would ensure it. I didn't wish to bring her here. It was duty that forced us to walk the club floors, not desire. But if she looked up at me with longing and need, if this place pulled a deep-seated fantasy from her that had to be fulfilled, I would not have the strength to deny her. Not here, with naked bodies writhing all around us.

If she needed, I would provide.

Because of this, the hope that she would need my hand, my mouth, my cock, eagerness filled my steps as we made our way to the final room, the last place we had to search. I'd chosen to save it as last for a reason.

If our prey were not here, it was the room where I would take our mate, bend her over a bench and mark her as mine for all the world to see. I wanted to show her off, to tell the planet, "She's mine."

Erik and Rolf had their fun with her, fucking her while I worked to solve this mystery. They'd given her pleasure and taken her body while I hunted. I would never deny them their pleasure in our mate, nor could I deny myself. And I found myself to be greedy indeed.

When we'd circled the room, I stopped and pulled her to stand before me. She looked up into my eyes and shook her head in answer to my unspoken question.

No.

He was not here.

The strain of the hunt left my body, replaced by a tension of a different sort. I lifted my hand to cup her cheek, eager to judge her reaction to my touch. Without evil lurking, I could focus on Sophia. I could turn this visit into something just for us. Yes, the place meant nothing to me any longer, the mark on my arm just a reminder of an empty past, but I could change that. I could take my mate here, connect with her in a way neither of us had imagined before.

Yes, I'd fucked her before, but she'd been surrounded

by all three of her mates. She'd surrendered first to Rolf, then Erik. Not to me.

I needed her to give herself to me. *Me*. The ache in my chest was new and unfamiliar, but I did not push it away. Instead, I let her see it in my eyes, the longing for her acceptance.

"Gunnar." She pressed her cheek into my palm before turning to place a kiss in the center. Her gaze returned to mine, soft and dark with desire. "I see the hunger in you."

"I want you, even here. Perhaps especially here," I added.

I leaned down and claimed her mouth in a kiss, crushing her cloaked body to mine. I knew she wore nothing beneath, and the knowledge burned through me like fire, making my cock heat and pulse to be free. To be inside her.

Panting when I released her, she stared up at me with a question in her eyes. I ignored everyone in the room, unnaturally aware of the bench directly to our left. The base was lined with new toys, plugs and dildos. Floggers and paddles, oil and wax as well. I could not deny the image burning into my mind of her naked and tied to that bench with her ass in the air as I spanked her, filled her ass and fucked her until she screamed.

"I'm not scared," she said, her voice barely above a whisper. I could see the thrumming beat of her pulse at her neck, knew that while she wasn't fearful, she was still nervous.

Now I was the one having difficulty controlling the air moving in and out of my lungs as I lowered my lips to her ear and whispered, "I want to take you over that bench and tie you down with everyone watching. I want to fill your ass and spank it, then fuck you until you scream."

"Yes, Sir."

"You want that here? This place... I'm going to fuck you, but it doesn't have to be here."

She looked up at me with her soft eyes, studying, assessing. "I want it. I want to see what you were like, what you are *still* like."

I shook my head as I stroked her cheek. "I'm not like this place anymore. I get what I need from you."

Nodding slightly, she continued. "And *I* get what I need from you. And I need you to do...whatever you want. Here."

She shivered before me and closed her eyes on a soft moan. With trembling fingers she reached for the tie at her neck and tugged at the knot. It gave away in a slow glide that held me hypnotized as the cloak fell to the floor in a pool of black, leaving her naked before me. Bare except for the decadent white shoes that forced her to walk with her hips thrust out. The spiked ends gave her added height and made her legs look even longer.

She stood before me with her head down, as I'd taught her, and whispered the words I'd heard a hundred times before. Never before had they made me feel so powerful and so vulnerable at the same time. This time, the words meant everything because they came from a woman who was truly mine, my mate. "Please, Sir. I want this. I want you."

"Fuck," I hissed through my teeth. My cock threatened to rip through my pants. "You can tell me to stop at any time."

"Yes, Sir."

I did not want to talk any longer. I grabbed her by the back of the neck and lifted her head so I could kiss her. I wasn't gentle, I didn't have it in me to be gentle. My cock flooded my body with lust, craving, need. I needed to fuck her. I needed to fill her with my seed and watch her writhe. I needed to conquer.

I kissed her a moment more and walked her to the bench, aligning the front of her hips with the padded rest that came to the front of her thighs. Hand still in her hair, I pushed her head down until she bent over the bench with her ass in the air.

"Raise your arms," I ordered.

Sophia lifted her arms above her head and I secured them using thick straps in place for just such a purpose. When she was secured on all fours, I reached down and released my hard cock from the uncomfortably tight black pants. Heavy with need, pre-cum already coated the tip. The essence of my cock would make her body eager and ready, but I didn't want to rely on seed power to seduce my mate. I needed her to look at me like that of her own accord.

I'd never worried about being desired. But I'd never imagined a mate of my own, a woman who would love me with every ounce of her heart and soul. And suddenly, I craved the love and acceptance of this woman I barely knew, needed her to want me like I needed air to breathe.

She made me weak, and yet, I could not walk away. This was obsession, not love. Primal need. I could not love her in return, the feeling long burned from my body by pain. I'd loved once, and lost everything.

I would not survive losing Sophia if I loved her.

Rolf and Erik could give her tender words and gentleness. But I could give her this. I would give us what we both needed.

Freedom from the cage of her mind. Freedom to experience total bliss beyond the limits set in place by guilt, shame or judgment. I would force her to give her pain to me, and I would drink it down like the greedy fuck I had become at first sight of her.

She flung her dark hair over her shoulder and looked up at me, licked her lips. I saw no fear in her eyes, only raw, naked lust. Watching her closely, I spoke slowly to be sure she understood every word.

"I'm going to spank your ass, mate, because I can. Because you enjoy the sting on your bare bottom. I'm going to make you burn, and then I'm going to fill that tight little ass so you'll be ready for Erik when next you see him."

She bit her lip and looked up at me. "What about you?"

The question was a dagger to my beating heart. *What about you?* No lover had ever asked what I wanted, what I needed. Not one. They took their pleasure as their due and walked away, sated and unconcerned of the cost to me to provide.

What about you?

Fuck. I was screwed.

I leaned over and grabbed a paddle from the supplies hanging off the bench and held it up for her inspection before stepping forward, close enough that she could take my cock into her mouth.

"Suck me, Sophia. Suck me so deep you can't breathe."

She opened her mouth and took me in, swirling her tongue around the head several times, licking my seed from the tip. I knew the moment the bonding essence in my seed hit her bloodstream. She moaned. Her eyes closing as she leaned forward. She sucked me down until my cock hit the back of her throat.

Gods. I'd never experienced such pleasure. She rubbed the base of my cock with her tongue, holding me in place. Sucking like she'd never get enough.

I threw my head back and fought off the orgasm drawing my balls into tight, painful spheres between my legs.

Her bare bottom called to me, so round and perfectly curved. So fucking beautiful.

Twisting, I reached beneath her and grabbed her nipple, twisting and pulling gently as I swung the paddle, bringing it down on her naked ass.

The crack of it filled the room, and left me feeling empty. Detached.

She jerked and cried out around my cock. I withdrew, forcing her to take a breath, but she shifted her head almost immediately, sucking me down once more. Her back arched, shoving her breast into my hand and raising her ass in the air for another hot strike of the paddle.

But I needed to feel her flesh, to connect with her as I never had with another. The paddle was an extension, something impersonal and distant, a way to keep my emotions separate from the act. For the first time in my life, I needed to feel connected. I needed this to be real.

I dropped the paddle and swung my open palm, relishing the feel of her soft flesh as I made her mine.

Smack!

Smack!

Smack!

A few club goers stopped to watch as I shifted my hips, carefully fucking her mouth as I spanked her ass a bright, fiery red.

Her soft cries turned to whimpers, then moans of need. I continued until she was writhing, pressing her hips forward, desperate for pressure on her clit, but the bench was unforgiving. She could not move, could only take what I gave her.

I stroked her gently, petting her back, her ass, as she continued to work me with her mouth. Forcing myself to focus on the elegant curve of her spine, the ripe roundness of her ass, instead of coming. Reaching over, I rubbed her tight rosette so she knew what was to come, but I moved on, plunged two fingers into her wet pussy.

With a gasp, she pressed back against my fingers, trying to fuck my hand, but still the restraints limited her movement and I denied her the one thing I knew she needed.

I would deny her until she broke, until she begged.

Slipping my cock from her hot, wet mouth, I moved to stand behind her, stroking the pink cheeks of her bare bottom with reverence. The skin was taut and hot, and I knew just the brush of my palm would be sensitive for her. This ass was mine. I could shove my cock in her if I wanted to. She remained lax and accepting of my touch, and I knew she would deny me nothing.

But I wanted my seed planted in her womb, my child growing in her body. Perhaps I'd done it the one time I'd fucked her. Perhaps Rolf or Erik had. Even though I shared her, I still wanted to mark her, own her, make sure she could never, ever leave me.

That fear rose up like a ghost from the grave and I shoved it away. Sophia was not part of my past, only stepping into it, into the club this one time. She was my future. A future I'd feared. A future I'd fought against until this moment.

I reached for the oil, coated my fingers and carefully worked my finger into her tight hole, coating her well, making sure she was ready for the plug I intended to place in her bottom. I watched her carefully, the way her hands clenched, her spine stiffened. The changing of her breath. The sheen of sweat that coated her flushed skin. When next we met Rolf and Erik, we would claim her in truth, all three of us—Erik in her ass, Rolf in her mouth and me in her hot, wet pussy. We'd fill her with seed, with our bonding essence, until she was well and truly ours. Addicted to our touch.

The effects of our seed power would wane in the coming weeks, but I needed her to belong to us fully before then, before her thirty days were up. She could still change her mind, find another mate on Viken per Brides Program protocol, but it was my job—no, all three of our jobs—to ensure that didn't happen. I wanted my child in her womb.

Before she could walk away from us.

Spreading her cheeks, I worked a chosen plug into her body with extreme patience, making sure I did not harm her. Her breathy pants were stunning, for this was new to her. I was pushing her and she was taking it beautifully.

When it was seated, I rubbed her weeping pussy with my cock, coated the broad head with her slick essence.

"Gunnar!" She flung her head back and forth, pressing her hips as far back as she could, trying to take me in. To be filled in her ass and pussy at the same time.

I smacked her ass with my bare hand and her back arched. "You do not make demands, Sophia." I pulled the plug out slowly before filling her again, fucking her ass the way I longed to fuck her pussy. I wrapped my fist around my cock and pumped once, twice, gathering the pre-cum from the tip. I slid my cum-coated fingers into her wet core and watched, waited with anticipation for her to react.

Her body bucked, her back lifting into the air as she writhed and begged me at last. "Please, Sir. Please fuck me. Please make me come."

"Ah, begging. I like to hear that."

Pleased now, I lined up my cock with her wet pussy and slid inside as a half dozen men and their subs watched from all around us. "Open your eyes, Sophia. Open your eyes and see how you are watched as I fuck you."

9

GUNNAR RUTTED INTO ME LIKE A CAVEMAN, HIS NEED primitive and carnal, and I welcomed each wild thrust of his hips. The plug he'd pressed into my bottom stretched me wide, his cock adding pressure to the brink of pain, pushing me higher and higher. I loved it. He knew, somehow, to push me past what I thought I could handle and into a new place where I loved it. I had no control, could only submit.

I'd thought I could suck his cock, swirl my tongue around that flared crown, but he hadn't wanted just that. He'd pushed himself farther and farther—albeit carefully—into my mouth. I'd had to breathe through my nose and concentrate, and yet he'd gone even farther, until he was touching the back of my throat. I hadn't been able to move, to push him away.

I'd had to take it, wanted to...and it had made my pussy weep, my nipples tighten. I'd needed it, that *possession,* along with the stinging smacks on my ass. God, pain had never felt so good.

He ordered me to open my eyes, and I did so reluctantly, until I saw the heated gazes of two Viken males and their women watching me with dark, lust-filled eyes.

They wanted what I had, those women. They wanted to be tied down and taken, dominated by their mates.

Some perhaps, even wanted Gunnar.

From the looks in the men's eyes, the women would get exactly what they desired—except for my mate.

He was mine. All mine. And I was his. Completely.

Gunnar bent over me, covering my back, his arms reaching underneath to tug and knead my breasts as his hips pounded into me from behind. Each thrust drove the plug a bit deeper as well, each retreat moving the object inside me as if two men fucked me, and I could not stop the image of riding Gunnar's cock as Erik filled me from behind.

I knew it would be Erik, for he'd already spoken of claiming my ass. That was his need, to take me there. His cock was hard and hot, and would fill me so deeply. I'd feel the hot spurts of his seed as he came. This plug, it was nothing in comparison to what I'd get from Erik.

I clenched my muscles around the plug as Gunnar's cock thrust deep, the tip touching my womb. The force sent a shock of pleasure-pain through my body on the inside, and my muscles collapsed beneath me as sensation overloaded my system. I could do nothing but take it. Nothing but let the others watch me give myself to my mate.

Gunnar buried his hand in my hair and stepped back, pulling me with him until my thighs came away from the bench and he could reach beneath me to stroke my clit. He slowed the movement of his cock and held my head back, my neck arched as he fucked me slowly. Every nerve ending deep inside flared to life. His cock missed not one inch of me. I wanted it fast and hard, but no. He was slowly torturing me. Taunting me. So fucking slow I thought I'd die of want.

"Gunnar, please," I begged again. I was not beyond begging. He'd turned me into a sweaty, needy mess and I didn't care.

"Come all over my cock, Sophia. Come now," he commanded.

He flicked my clit fast and thrust deep and I screamed as the orgasm rushed through me.

Gunnar did not stop moving. He did not release me. He pushed me to another release before I'd had time to recover from the first. When I finally stilled, my pussy so swollen and sensitive every thrust of his hard cock a sensual glide making me quiver and burn for him, he released me.

I fell forward, slack and accepting of anything he wanted from me. I gave myself into his care, completely sated and warm, content. The others could watch, but they meant nothing. It was just Gunnar and me. I needed to please him now, reveled in the power of my body to push him to such primitive lusts, such mindless need.

He took his time—still—riding me, using my body, filling and pushing me out of satiation to need once again. He built the fire slowly this time, the bulbous head of his cock like a ridge of pleasure as he pushed into my wet, swollen and sensitive pussy, pulled out.

His cock swelled and hard hands grabbed my hips. His pacing increased and I knew he was about to come, to fill me with his seed.

And I wanted it all, every drop. I wanted to own him as he owned me, to know that I carried a piece of him inside me. I never wanted to lose that connection, to be without my mates.

Gripping my hips in an almost brutal hold, he came, his cock jumping and pulsing inside my core, filling me with his essence, his seed power. I welcomed the rush of heat I knew would follow. Seconds later, the chemical in his seed rushed through my bloodstream like the sweetest fire, and my pussy responded, clenching and spasming around his hard length as another orgasm made me moan and shake, the rush indescribable, the bond so strong I closed my eyes for fear I would reveal too much to those who still watched him conquer me, body and soul.

When it was over, he gently removed the plug and wiped my body with cleaning clothes and scented oil before releasing me and draping the cloak back over my shoulders. With a sigh, I lifted my arms to his chest and raised my face for a kiss. For once, confident that he would not deny me.

Before this moment, Gunnar had been the great unknown for me. Rolf was witty and hid the pain of his past with humor and wit. Erik loved to brood, but he did not carry darkness the way Gunnar did. Erik would release it into the world, would rant or bellow, allowing me to soothe him. In just two days, I'd learned my men and grown fond of them.

But Gunnar had been walking darkness. Impossible to read, impossible to know. I knew his protective streak, but nothing more. But a woman can learn much from a lover's touch, and now I knew Gunnar's secret.

I believed that he loved me, whether he was ready to admit it or not. He cherished me. He would move heaven or hell to protect me. His darkness chipped away at his soul, the loneliness he carried like a shield to his heart tried to hide him from me. But it was too late. He touched me, and I knew.

But I would be patient. Rolf's easy banter hid an aching heart. Erik's gruff demands his fear of losing me, of watching me die the way he'd been forced to watch his family perish. Despite their dark pasts, of all my mates, Gunnar was the most afraid of what loving me might do to him. Erik and Rolf had both loved, been loved. But to Gunnar, loving me was the ultimate vulnerability, a weakness he'd never allowed himself before. A leap he'd never taken because his love would be all consuming, powerful and obsessive.

Erik and Rolf would love me, pamper me, push me to reveal my needs, my darkest secrets. But Gunnar's love could break us both open and drown us. Deep down, in the most instinctive and passionate core of my soul, I understood this about him in a way that I couldn't explain.

And so I reached for him now, when the fury of his hard cock thrusting into my body was done, because I sensed he needed to be reassured that he had not broken me, had not frightened me away. Not with being at the club, or with others watching. No, Gunnar feared my reaction to *him*, to his carnal nature. On the contrary...

"Gunnar."

He looked down into my eyes and I did not ask permission, not for this. I reached up and buried my hands in his hair, pulling him down for a kiss.

The kiss was not wild or full of passion, but gentle, tender, a thank-you I could not speak aloud because I did not believe he would be ready to hear my words. But a kiss could not be denied. And so, I would thank him with the gentle press of my lips to his, the trusting embrace of my small frame.

He did not pull away, but lingered beneath my gentleness and I knew I'd been right. He needed this side of me as much as he needed my body riding his cock. He needed to be loved.

After long moments, I released him and stepped back. "That was...incredible, but we did not find what we sought."

I saw his eyes change then, seeing as he, too, remembered our true mission. A good fucking had certainly cleared both our minds of everything else. For a few, fabulous minutes, I'd not been worried about anything but the hard length of Gunnar's cock filling me, the sharp sting of his palm on my ass, the carnal press of him filling my body with his seed.

"No, we did not. Perhaps next time." I could see and feel the tenseness returning to his body in the stiffness of his shoulders, the grim set of his jaw. We'd have to return, over and over, until we found the man we sought. The future of the entire planet rested on my shoulders. And as strange as that seemed, I was glad they'd accidentally abducted me during transport. Glad everything had worked out the way it had.

And if I had to return to this club every day for a year and allow Gunnar to fuck my brains out with an audience, well, that was a sacrifice I was willing to make. In fact, my body trembled with excitement and anticipation at the remembered feel of Gunnar's dominant touch. The hunt for a killer made me so tense, my body so hyped up on adrenaline and nerves, that the orgasm had been like a fucking nuclear explosion in my system. I'd short-circuited, my brain shut down.

Gunnar was like my personal EMP.

"Take me home, Gunnar." I needed to be home, surrounded by my mates. Safe. God, I just wanted to be able to relax and let them hold me. I was so tired. The rush of the hunt for the VSS henchman had long since faded. And Gunnar's expert and skilled fucking wore me out, emotionally and physically. I just wanted to go home, and on this strange new planet, home was wherever my men were. All three of them.

"Gladly, mate." His eyes had changed, the dark color softened, the mask gone, allowing me to see the gentleness he tried so hard to hide from the world. I was looking straight into his soul, and I fell in love with him, hard and fast, in that moment.

He was mine, and I was never going to let him go.

Gunnar took my hand and led me to the entrance. I ignored everyone around me, focused on the feel of his strong hand around mine as he escorted me to the door. My body was lax and sated, the seed power now floating in my bloodstream made me feel languid and content. Happy.

That was what this was. Happiness. Contentment. Two things I hadn't felt in months.

No, years. Since my mother's cancer first appeared and I'd made a deal with the devil in the form of Anthony Corelli.

Body sated, I wondered at the other women in the club. "Is everyone here mated? What happens to females who crave more...you know, and they don't have a mate?" The sated feeling of my mates' seed seeping into my system made me curious. What happened to women who only got one taste?

"A male of honor would not take a female without preventing such a bonding. Casual sex is not forbidden, but the males are trusted to take special medication to prevent the bonding."

"Did you take that medication?" I asked.

His look was pure male possession. "No, mate. I very much want you to crave my touch."

Well, that wasn't a problem. I craved my men. All three of them. Constantly.

Even through my pleasure-induced haze, duty forced me to listen to the voices around us, and so I did, relieved when the man I'd been looking for did not make an appearance as we reached the entrance. Our visit had been a waste. Well, perhaps not, for Gunnar and I had connected in a way we might not have if we were anywhere else.

Gunnar paused before the door, the question in his eyes, and I shook my head. No. I had not heard the voice we sought.

We were steps away from the door when it opened and a Viken man and his female friend walked inside.

They talked and joked, and I shook my head once more. No. Not him.

The door did not close and I peeked around Gunnar's shoulder to see another man and woman outside, courteously holding the door for us.

Gunnar stepped through and I followed a step behind him, as was expected from a submissive at the club. As I passed the open door, I thanked the Viken male automatically.

"My pleasure."

I stiffened instantly, a chill racing the length of my spine as I remembered that deep timbre saying something else entirely.

If she's not royalty, or worth a ransom, kill her.

It was *him*. Oh, God. Fear and panic rushed to the front of my mind and I grabbed the side of Gunnar's uniform with rigid fingers. That voice.

I glanced over at the man's wrist where he held the door open.

Yes. There it was. The tattoo.

This was the man we'd been hunting, the man who'd tried to kill the Queen, the man who'd nearly cost me my life.

———

Gunnar

I sensed Sophia as she lagged behind, stumbling into my side. Her hand grasped at my shirt with urgency, all softness gone from her. We stood just outside the entry, the cool air refreshing after the cloying scents of fucking from the club. I should have been relaxed, pleased with my mate, but my contentment washed away the second I understood her actions.

My prey stood before me, a man I knew all too well. The Viken who held the door for us.

The couple had yet to go inside as they were staring at us in return where we'd frozen in place. The female wore a cloak identical to Sophia's, the hood pulled up to hide her features. I could only see the lower half of her face beneath the hood. I assessed her bowed head, the hands folded before her as her companion led her into the club by a long silver chain affixed to a collar around her neck.

No, she was not the threat. The slave female was not who concerned me. It was *him*.

Dorn.

"Gunnar, it has been a long time. I am surprised to see you here."

Sophia's hand moved to the back of my shirt, her fingers curling and digging into my skin.

The man who had wanted my mate dead stood before me, and I couldn't do a damn thing about it. Not here. Not now.

"Dorn." I said his name in a flat tone, the best I could manage when the urge to wrap my hands around his neck and strangle the life from his worthless body flooded me.

The man was my height, yet his body was not honed from fighting, from battle. He was thin and lithe, and unchanged in the long years since last I'd seen him. I easily outweighed him by fifty pounds, but I did not doubt his speed, agility or ruthlessness. His black hair and eyes matched his soul, his sneer, his cruel nature. I'd seen him with females inside the club many, many times. Based on the slave collar around his lover's neck, I guessed not much had changed.

I'd watched him break many, men and women both, watched them writhe and scream, cry and beg him to stop.

He never did, not until he was ready. Not until he'd broken them wide open, pushed them past the point they'd wished to go.

I'd cringed the first few times I'd witnessed his calculated and expert cruelty. But my mentor had instructed me to watch and learn, and so I had. And been shocked to see the people he hurt come back time and again, begging him for more. Begging him to break them.

Pain was never my thing, but I understood it. He excelled at dealing out pain, and many at the club fought to serve him, to experience a taste of his lash or cane. There was no personal connection between Dorn and the women who served him, only pain meted out for his pleasure. He was a Sadist in the truest form. I should have been surprised that I'd spent so much time in years past with the man who would betray the three Kings, the man who would stoop so low as to murder a beautiful woman and an innocent child.

However, I did not doubt for an instant that Sophia's identification was accurate. If anyone could plot murder with icy precision, it was Dorn.

We'd both been members of the club for years. I'd gone off to fight the Hive and serve Viken, he working as a civil servant, moving his way up the ranks in government. I didn't know what his title was now, but he'd always been an arrogant ass. I knew he'd have a mark of rank on his body somewhere. He always wore his status like armor, and wielded his influence like a weapon.

He held out his arm for a warrior's greeting and we locked forearms the same way we'd done hundreds of times before. I glanced quickly to his hand where it gripped my arm and found exactly what I was looking for, a signet ring.

On his middle finger was a large ring, a black arrow on gold, the symbol of a council member from Sector Two.

Fuck. He wasn't just ambitious. If he'd made it to the council, he had wealth and influence. Connections. He wasn't just a sadistic ass, he was dangerous. Fuck.

I'd have to kill him.

When all was said and done, when the interrogations were over, I'd have to make sure he was well and truly ended. He posed too big a threat to my mate if allowed to live. I knew the three Kings would agree, worried for their own mate and child. At the moment, I wasn't a servant of the Kings, I was a man. And this asshole had ordered someone to kill Sophia.

I lifted my gaze from the ring and met his prideful gaze with carefully banked fury. Sophia was safely behind me, but I had no doubt things would become critical the moment he saw her face.

Sophia was too beautiful, to perfect to escape his notice for long. And he was a predictable bastard in one way at least, he never forgot a beautiful woman.

"I see you climbed the ranks to a seat on the council."

"And I see that you survived war with the Hive." The

voice grated on my nerves, I wondered how Sophia would react, if she would tremble with remembered fear or panic, if the sound of his voice made her heart race and terror invade her limbs.

His gaze flicked to Sophia. Out of the corner of my eye, I saw that her hood was not up, that if Dorn took one step to his left, he would see her fully. Turning, I flicked the material up and over her, shielding her from the man's sight even as I reached behind me and moved her to stand completely behind my back, out of his reach.

The decision to walk away made my blood burn like acid, but I would not face him here, not with Sophia by my side. I refused to place my mate in danger. Now that I knew who he was, he would be dealt with. He was a high-ranking council member in Sector Two, but the three Kings would not allow council politics to stand in their way. Two was my sector, King Lev's sector. Sector Two was famous for brutal efficiency in its warriors, for men who liked to be in control.

Lev's fury would equal mine. Neither of us would permit this bastard to live long.

For now, I needed to get my mate as far away from him as possible. For now, I had to tread carefully.

"Yes. I'm lucky," I replied. "If you'll excuse us, we are tired. The third floor was as entertaining as I remembered."

"Of course." He inclined his head and I gave the couple a brief nod, then took Sophia's arm and pulled her along next to me as I walked down the street. She was stiff and slow, as if her legs were numb, for I had to tug her along behind me. It was as if Dorn's voice triggered a deep fear in her, or sent her back into shock. I tucked her under my arm and tried to will my heat, my strength into her small body. "I've got you, mate. He'll never threaten you again, I swear it."

She shivered in response to my words, but picked up the pace, clinging to my side. Once we rounded a corner out of sight from the entrance, I stopped and turned her to face me. The sky was dark, but the city lights made the street bright. People were about, walking to their homes, their places of work. Their lives. Innocent people streamed past us as I processed the truth.

The VSS had infiltrated the sector councils. The three Kings had feared the movement had recruited spies and conspirators from deep within the government. I suspected this would be the case, but there had been no proof. Until now. Until Dorn.

Leaning down, I looked into her eyes from beneath the edge of the hood.

"Do not be afraid."

She licked her lips. Only a short time ago, I'd have found that innocent gesture arousing. Now, with her eyes wide with fear and anxiety, I saw it as an outlet of her nerves.

"He...it was him. I...why did you let him go?"

"He won't get away, I promise. I know who he is now, thanks to you. He won't escape justice. Breathe, Sophia." I placed my hands on either shoulder and pulled her close. She melted into me, accepting my protection and strength, trusting me to keep her safe, and my heart swelled with a painful ache I'd not felt in a long, long time. Her faith humbled me, made me feel complete, filled a void in me I hadn't realized was empty. And I vowed to be worthy, to protect my beautiful little mate to my last dying breath.

She pulled away and looked up at me, her warm eyes clouded with confusion. "You know him? Is he your friend?" she asked, her voice stronger.

I nodded once, my jaw clenched. "He's not my friend. I've known him for a long time. He's belonged to Club Trinity even longer than I. He was one of my trainers in the Masters program there."

Sophia closed her eyes and shuddered in revulsion. "God, how could any woman let him touch her?"

"He's a Sadist, and very good at what he does. For those that find release through pain, he's exactly what they need."

She opened her eyes and blinked slowly. Once. Twice, as my words processed. "So, he likes hurting people?"

I sighed, unsure if she could ever understand the complexities of need Club Trinity catered to. "Some people enjoy pain, little one."

"I know. It's the same on Earth. I just..."

"What is it?"

"He's—he's evil, Gunnar. Pure evil." She buried her face in my chest and I wrapped my arms around her, provided a safe place for her to release her anger and fear. "He was going to kill Leah and Allayna. He wanted that other man to kill me. He didn't hesitate. He talked about killing me like he was stepping on a spider."

I rubbed her back until her shivering stopped. "Let's get out of here and go tell the others. The Kings will take care of arresting him. And when they're done with him, Lev will kill him."

She shook her head in denial and I placed my hands

under her chin, gently lifted her face and forced her to meet my gaze. "If Lev doesn't kill him, I will. He'll never threaten you again."

"It's just like on Earth," she replied. "It's like I never left."

"Why do you say this?" I knew little about the far-off planet, but I recognized the resignation, the sound of defeat in my mate's voice, and I did not like it.

"There are many names for groups like the VSS. Terrorists. Mafia. Cartels. Gangs. The title is irrelevant, but there's always a leader, someone with...minions beneath, and more foot soldiers and pawns beneath them. It's like roots on a tree, they spread out and permeate every aspect of society. Government, police, banking, everything. The people on the bottom are expendable, and so are those in the middle. But those at the top are protected at any cost. It's vicious and cruel and no one is safe. And you never know who to trust, and who's been bought."

"Yes," I replied. "That sounds quite similar to the VSS."

"That is how I was put in jail. I was at the bottom. I was expendable. That guy, Dorn, is he at the bottom?" she asked.

"No, I'm afraid not. He sits on the council in Sector Two. He has risen to a position of power."

She shuddered, her eyes clouded with worry. Unable to resist offering comfort, I stroked her cheek. "Do not fear, mate. I will take care of this. You've done your part."

"Yes," a voice said from behind me. "She has been a very busy little thing."

Grabbing Sophia, I spun to face our enemy and pushed her behind me.

"Dorn." I greeted him through clenched teeth, wondering exactly how much he'd overheard.

He stood there, the lighting casting shadow over his face, his female beside him. Her face was still covered by her hood, her posture that of a true submissive. Dorn leaned down and murmured to his female. She nodded beneath her hood and turned and walked back in the direction of the club.

Dorn lifted his head and returned his attention to me. "You have taken a mate, Gunnar. Congratulations."

I shrugged with a casualness that hid my anger. I didn't want the bastard anywhere near Sophia.

"It seems the Kings are pleased with their Earth bride as well," Dorn said.

"How did you know she was from Earth?" I countered. Females on Viken were quite similar in appearance to those from Earth. Unlike planet Xerima, where the females were tall and strong and fiercely muscled, their women as likely to kill a man as ride his cock, Sophia's softness blended in readily enough. We had not announced that we had a mate, nor that she had come from Earth. Only those in the transport centers and the guards that surrounded the royal family knew of the match.

And Dorn. Because he'd been the one to have the transports crossed. Because he was the one who'd wanted her dead. And discovered her anything but.

"My position allows me access to quite a bit of data."

I couldn't allow Sophia to remain. Dorn's cover was blown. The only way for him to survive now was to kill me and Sophia both. If I could distract him, stand between him and my mate, she should be able to make it. "Go back to the club, Sophia. Summon Erik and wait for me there."

When I gave her a little shove between her shoulder blades to get her moving, Dorn waited calmly, acting as if he would allow her to waltz right past him.

When she was just out of reach, he pulled an ion pistol from inside his coat and pointed it at me. "Sophia, is it?"

Sophia froze in place, her eyes wide with terror as she looked from the blaster to me and back again. "Yes."

"Come here. Now. Or Gunnar is a dead man."

I saw the battle take place behind her eyes. "No, Sophia. Just run. Go."

She bit her lip, that nervous habit I found so endearing, and stepped to place her chest directly in front of the ion pistol. "Leave Gunnar out of this, Dorn. It's between you and me."

Dorn grabbed her by the arm, spun her around and pressed the blaster to the side of her head. "Women are always so stupid, Sophia. This was never about you. This is about saving Viken."

As Dorn pressed the tip of the ion pistol to Sophia's forehead, I saw her flinch in pain, but she made no sound. Her gaze caught mine and the resignation I saw there scared me more than the pistol. She was going to do something stupid to try to save me. I could see it in her eyes, in the stiff set of her shoulders and the stubborn line of her beautiful chin.

She'd been used by men just like Dorn on Earth, and I saw the resolve in her, the rage.

And it terrified me.

I held out my hands, more to plead with my mate than with the man holding her. "Don't do anything stupid. We can talk about this."

Dorn laughed, the sound hollow and without mirth. "Talk, Gunnar? The VSS is through talking. The Kings need to die. They've disrupted centuries of honor and tradition."

"It's not about honor for you, Dorn. It's about power. I've known your family my entire life. The old line of kings."

Dorn interrupted, "The rightful rulers of Viken. The child Queen has no right to usurp our claim. She's an alien child born of an alien mother." Leaning down, he buried his nose in Sophia's hair, breathing in her sweet scent. "Like this alien bitch here."

Dorn shook her and pulled on her hair until she winced, crying out in pain. Rage rose like a monster within me at the strain etched on her face, at the sick enjoyment I saw on his.

Sophia was the only thing that mattered to me. In that moment I realized just how completely she had won my heart.

Without her, life was meaningless.

Sophia must live. Dorn? He would die, right here, right now, even if he took me with him.

10

I was a pawn. Dorn, the fucker, wanted me dead because I'd accidentally seen too much. I was the loose thread that was ruining his carefully hidden life as a member of the VSS. This entire fucked-up situation was just like what happened back home with the Corellis. They'd given me no choice but to smuggle for them. I knew their faces, knew their crimes—my crimes—and could put them all away.

To keep me from identifying them, I'd been the one turned in to the FBI, the one who'd been caught red-handed, found guilty and sentenced to prison. Not them. It didn't matter that I'd been innocent of everything but wanting to save my mother's life. Once I'd taken the money for my mother's medical treatment, they'd owned me. Used me. And when my mother was gone, they'd held my own life, my freedom, the lives of my cousins over my head. I'd taken the money to save my mother, not realizing that I'd sold my soul in the process.

And so I had done whatever they wanted me to do. Smuggle. Lie. Again and again. Until I was caught. Then I was tossed away, convicted.

I realized, with Dorn's space gun at my head, that if I'd stayed on Earth, I'd most likely be dead. Even in jail, my knowledge would have been a liability to the Corellis. Surely they had someone on the inside who would have been able to kill me. To eliminate the threat.

Just as Dorn was doing now. Once I was dead, and Gunnar with me, Dorn was a free man.

I could feel the tension vibrating from Dorn's body. The energy coming from him made me think of a wild animal, hurt and cornered. Desperate. Willing to gnaw off its own foot to escape the trap.

"Say goodbye," he hissed.

I took one last look at Gunnar, his face handsome, even etched with anger and fear. He was perfect, everything I wanted in a mate. In one of my mates. I held his gaze as I felt the pistol pressed into my forehead, resolved to what I must do. I had to save him at any cost. If I could buy Gunnar a few seconds, that would be all he needed to reach Dorn, to stop him.

"Gunnar," I said, my voice shaky. "I...I love you."

Dorn laughed. "So perfect."

I held my breath as I knew the shot would come at any moment. I was out of time.

Gunnar jumped toward us as I rammed my elbow into Dorn's gut and slammed my heel down on his instep.

"Cunt!" Dorn yelled at me as I slammed my head

back into his chin as hard as I could and fought his hold on the pistol. I wrapped my hands around his large wrist and put every ounce of strength I had into shoving the gun away from my head.

The weapon fired. The strange light blasted right past my face and hit the wall of the building closest to us. Across the street, people screamed and scrambled to get away.

I wrenched free of Dorn's hold just as Gunnar reached me, throwing me to the ground under his massive frame. He covered me as I heard another shot fire, hitting the ground inches from Gunnar's head.

"Gunnar!" I screamed his name and tried to get him off me as I heard another strange buzzing sound.

Gunnar tensed at the sound. "Fuck, stay down!"

More afraid of the urgency in Gunnar's command, I huddled as he rose to charge Dorn.

I rolled onto my side as Gunnar charged our enemy. He was within a few steps. Dorn lifted the gun he had and aimed at my mate with a look of pure malice twisting his features into a cruel mask of hatred.

An odd blasting sound, then a weird sizzle shocked me motionless. I flinched after seeing Gunnar's eyes widen, afraid he'd been shot. I tightened every muscle in my body, assessing the situation as I rolled onto my hands and knees to rush Dorn. I would not let my mate die at the hands of someone so vile, so corrupt. Gunnar deserved so much better than that.

Dorn's hold on his gun slackened, then fell away, the gun clattering on the hard ground at his feet. I blinked in confusion as I watched him slump to the ground. Confused, I looked up and discovered half of his face gone, a gruesome and charred mess of bone and flesh and exposed brain made me moan. I rolled onto my side, gagging, the contents of my stomach churned and spewed as I closed my eyes, the image of his death burned onto my retinas until I could not escape the sight.

Gunnar launched himself at me. Faster than I could process, Gunnar lifted me and sprinted around the corner, away from Dorn. Gunnar pressed me against the wall of the nearest building, blocking my body with his own.

"What...happened?" I asked, my brain confused, my heart pumping.

"Sniper," Gunnar bit out.

He looked over his shoulder, pressed his communication device. "Get down here. Now. We've got a sniper shooting at Sophia."

"On our way." Erik's voice came through the speaker on Gunnar's wrist, his calm assurance helped me breathe. Erik must have ended the call because Gunnar didn't speak further.

"Don't move," he said when I tried to wiggle away. The wall was unforgiving against my back, Gunnar's hard body unyielding at my front. "Someone's fucking shooting!"

Anyone left on the street had fled before, but the single shot and the dead body ensured everyone stayed away.

I shook my head. "No. You're wrong, Gunnar. We're safe now. I'm safe."

"What the fuck are you talking about? See Dorn? He's missing half his head. We're not going out there."

"It was the VSS," I said.

"Dorn worked for the VSS."

I shook my head. It all made complete sense, at least to me. "Not anymore. His cover was blown. They killed him. He was a liability."

Gunnar was in warrior mode. His senses heightened, his body ready to fight. He'd been helpless standing there with Dorn holding me hostage. He'd had no weapon, no way to save me. That helplessness was gone now.

"Sophia, what the fuck are you talking about?"

I knew his tone wasn't truly focused on me. He had to see past the dead body and think, but he was too riled. And I had no doubt it was because of me. I was his weakness here, his Achilles' heel.

Taking hold of his chin, I forced him to look at me. Only when his dark eyes held mine did I speak. "As soon as we identified him, as soon as they knew I was alive, Dorn became a liability for the VSS."

Gunnar looked down at me, but some of the stiffness left him. "Now that he's dead, you can't hurt the VSS."

"Right. I'm nobody, Gunnar. Trust me. I know how these people operate. I'm worthless to them. And now that Dorn is dead, I'm not even worth the effort or energy to kill." I sighed, closing my eyes and imagined a black ops sniper in the movies back home. "Whoever took the shot is long gone. As soon as he killed Dorn, he would vanish like a ghost."

Gunnar shifted and I opened my eyes to see him inspecting the sidewalk behind us, leaning out to look up at the windows on the buildings, the rooflines.

"See anything?" I asked.

"No. Your logic is sound, Sophia." He turned back to me and lifted his arms to the wall on either side of my head, caging me. "But I'm not letting you go until Erik and Rolf arrive. I can't take the chance."

I didn't argue or struggle, simply leaned forward and plastered my body to my mate's much larger, stronger frame, eager for the comfort he offered. Even if the sniper was gone, the adrenaline pumping through my body made me shake. I knew it would take a long time for me to process this, to get the image of Dorn's death out of my mind. But relief rushed through me, making my knees weak. I was safe now. No one out there trying to kill me.

I could just be a mate, a normal citizen. A big, fat nobody.

I lifted my hand so I could rasp my thumb over his whiskers.

"I guess I'll have to thank the Corellis." I gave a small smile, knowing how lucky I'd been to leave Earth. "I'm sure they don't even think about me anymore. But thanks to them, I was mated to some crazy space alien I adore."

That got Gunnar's attention and he pulled far enough away to press his forehead to mine. "You said you loved me, mate."

Lifting both hands to his face, I held him to make sure he felt my touch. I wanted him to feel my words, too, all the way down to his soul. "I love you, Gunnar. I know it's crazy, and too fast, and totally illogical, but..."

Gunnar shut me up with a kiss that curled my toes. I wrapped my arms around his head and held on tight as he pulled me close and made me forget all about the last few minutes of hell.

"Gunnar!" Erik shouted.

Gunnar stepped away then, and I took a deep breath. Before me was Erik, Rolf standing over Dorn's dead body with a host of guards. Royal guards swarmed both sides of the street, running into buildings and shining searchlights down alleyways and into dark corners. Both Erik and Rolf wore their Viken United guard uniforms, complete with weapons and the light body armor I'd come to recognize.

After a minute, Rolf came to stand beside us, the entire time his pistol was up, his gaze searching the buildings around us.

"Sophia is safe now," Gunnar said. "And the sniper is long gone."

Both men frowned and didn't stand down.

"Explain it to them, Sophia," Gunnar ordered.

All three men glanced at me, but once I started speaking, telling Erik and Rolf what I'd said to Gunnar, they remained vigilant.

"The VSS only cared about eliminating Dorn. Not me. He'd been identified. He was the liability. I was just a stupid mistake," I insisted.

"But you can implicate them," Erik said, lowering his weapon.

"No. I could only implicate Dorn. The VSS has no reason to kill me now. Unless they kill for sport, I'm safe. They won't want anything to do with me."

"It makes sense," Rolf said, pulling me in for a hug. I felt the frantic beat of his heart as he held me. He was warm and I reveled in his familiar scent.

"So the VSS continues. We've done nothing to bring them down," Erik said, disappointed.

"No, they lost a high-ranking council member from Sector Two. And we're free," Gunnar said. "Sophia is safe."

Rolf passed me to Erik, who also held me close. "That scared ten years off my life."

Gunnar grunted his agreement.

The men stood around me in a protective circle. People started to come out from hiding, voices speaking, someone loomed over the body until a member of the Royal Guard chased him off and set up a perimeter. I ignored them all. I didn't care what they did. I had my men. We were safe once and for all. The VSS might continue to be a scourge on Viken, but it was not my fight, at least not right now. I didn't have a target on my back any longer.

"Can we go home now?" I asked.

"Yes," Gunnar answered. "We'll have you home as soon as possible."

"Didn't you have me just a little while ago?" I asked, teasing.

"You didn't have me," Rolf replied.

"Or me," Erik added, raising his brows. "What did Gunnar do to you in there? I want a detailed account, mate, and I want you to tell me every naughty detail."

That was Erik, talking dirty. My pussy and bottom clenched, remembering. "He...he prepared me for all three of you."

Erik growled. "For us to claim you together?"

I nodded.

"Then you accept us as your mates? No second doubts? No denial?"

Rolf stroked a finger down my cheek. Erik's hands were on my shoulders. Gunnar didn't touch me, but his eyes were filled with lust.

But he would touch me, fill me, fuck me. I wanted all of them.

"Yes, I accept all three of you as my mates. I want you to take me home and make me forget everything but you."

———

Eric

ROLF AND I HAD BEEN PACING, WAITING. WE'D TRIED TO relax, but it had been impossible. Sure, Gunnar would keep her safe, would definitely fuck her while they were in the club, but time seemed to have moved at a glacial pace. When he'd reached us through the InterCom, we'd sighed in relief. But that had been short lived.

Holy fuck.

We've got a sniper shooting at Sophia.

Those were not words we expected to hear, nor in Gunnar's slightly frantic tone. We'd never heard him *frantic* before. It wasn't a word I'd ever use to describe him. Ever.

But now, with Sophia in danger, it was bad. We'd only just found her, our mate, from all the planets in the universe. She'd been miraculously matched to the three of us and now her life was threatened. Again.

We'd leapt over furniture, knocked down people who were in our way to get to them. It took ten interminable minutes to cross Central City and find them. We couldn't miss the flurry of Vikens leaving the area. People talking about someone being shot, a dead body, had us running even faster. Then we saw the body sprawled on the ground, blood pooling thick and dark on the street. It wasn't Sophia. Nor Gunnar.

Relief pumped through my veins. It wasn't our mate. It wasn't Gunnar. That didn't mean they were safe. Fuck, we didn't even know if the dead Viken was Sophia's mystery man.

We had no idea who he was, but half of his face was gone. Had Gunnar shot him up close?

We didn't linger since there was no question he was not a danger any longer, only raised our own ion pistols and searched for any others.

And when we found Gunnar and Sophia, my heart finally settled. Shit, I'd never been so scared in my life, and I'd spent years fighting the Hive. Just imagining what had happened to Sophia was enough to put me off a warrior's life permanently. I was getting too old for this shit. It was time to settle down to a sedate life as a royal guard and come home to fuck our mate for the rest of our lives. Perhaps fill her with a baby or two. A little girl who looked just like Sophia, but first a boy to protect her. As if three Viken warrior fathers weren't enough.

I glanced at Rolf, saw the relief in every line of his body, too.

Gunnar had quickly confirmed the dead body was the "voice", but learning it had been Dorn made me furious. I knew who he was, had met him a time or two, but hadn't had the connection of the club with him like Gunnar.

And after hearing what had happened, I knew the VSS was more insidious than we ever imagined. We couldn't bring it down in one day. It was a network of evil, creating an ever-growing web that spread through the government, the communities and even the Sectors. We could slow it, and perhaps with Dorn's death, we had, but it wasn't over. Like the Hive, the battle would go on.

As for Sophia, her words rung true. She was safe, at least from the VSS. They wouldn't draw any further attention to themselves for her. She wasn't worth it. Not with three royal guards as mates. Not with Dorn dead. While she wasn't any safer than anyone else on Viken from the VSS's threats, she wasn't a target any longer.

It was time to make her ours. She wanted it. I needed it. I hadn't thought much about her thirty-day decision period. I just assumed if she had been matched to three Vikens, surely there were no more good matches. We were it for her. I knew it and now she did as well. It was time to make her ours.

I'd never imagined I'd have a second family. No, Gunnar and Rolf weren't brothers by birth, but we were ones nonetheless, bound together by battle, by honor, by Sophia.

Sophia.

She was the one who made our family. Without her, we were three warriors. Yes, brothers. But now we were mates, lovers, protectors. She belonged to us, just as we belonged to her. There would be no separating us now. And as soon as we had her alone, we'd claim her completely. The bond would be permanent.

———

ROLF

· · ·

BACK AT OUR QUARTERS, SAFE WITHIN THE ROYAL FORTRESS at Viken United, I'd taken Sophia straight to the medical station, despite her insistence that she was not hurt. I growled every time the doctor put a hand on her, even if it had been a clinical touch. The smirk on the older Viken's face told me he'd found my possessiveness humorous.

We hadn't told him about Dorn or the VSS. If we had, the man surely wouldn't be smiling.

Only when the doctor assured me she was all right had I taken her back to our quarters and straight into the bathing room where I stripped her bare and took her into the tub. I didn't speak, at least not much more than single-word directions. I couldn't. I hadn't settled yet. I was the calm one of her trio of mates, but in this moment, I was unsettled. It had been too close, her demise. Again. In the short time she'd been on Viken, she'd had more danger than many Vikens citizens who lived here their entire lives.

And yet Sophia wasn't a warrior. She wasn't even Viken. She was a petite, smart, sassy, willful alien, but she'd taken on the VSS and survived. Twice, and neither time had I been there to defend her. Even Gunnar, the most ruthless of us, had been helpless.

And that was two times too many. And so I tried to ease my fears. It was over. She was safe. The VSS would not come after her, as she'd said. She was just a Viken bride now. Nothing more. And thank fuck for that.

It was now time to remind her of that, of the reason she'd been matched in the first place. She *was* our bride and tonight we would claim her together.

This time, the bath was more clinical than romantic.

It had only been a day since we'd shared one before and yet so much had changed. I cleaned her body of every bit of dirt, of blood, and hopefully, in a way, her mind, of what had happened.

She wanted to be claimed by us, and we needed her fully ready. She'd said she was when we were out on the street, Dorn's body sprawled behind us, but the adrenaline had worn off for all of us. Yes, the relief was palpable, but so were the memories.

It was my job, while Gunnar and Erik bathed elsewhere, to ease the worries from Sophia.

"I'm fine, Rolf," she'd said, taking the soap from me. I'd washed her twice and apparently I was the one still upset. *She* was soothing *me*.

Using her finger to indicate I turn around, I did so. She washed my back and I groaned. The feel of her small hands was enticing. Knowing she was safe and whole and cleaning my back was like a balm to my fear.

"You had a trauma," I told her, enjoying the way her fingers played over my shoulders.

"I've had a trauma for the past two years," she replied. "It all started when my mother became sick, when she needed the expensive medicine. But no more. No more pain and suffering. No more bad guys. I'm ready for the future. Not the past. That's what my mother would want. That's what *I* want."

I turned around and took her hands, looked at her dark eyes. She looked different with her hair slicked back. Simple. Pure. Perfect.

"You aren't planning on fucking her all by yourself, are you?" Erik asked, naked as the day he was born, arms crossed. He and Gunnar stood beside the tub, grins on their faces.

We glanced up at them and I couldn't miss the easy smile on Sophia's face.

"All three of us are her mates. He doesn't have enough cocks to do it," Gunnar added. It was good to hear the teasing tone in his voice.

I grinned. "I could find a way."

Sophia laughed and the sound eased something raw in me. Erik and Gunnar eased as well.

Perhaps it wasn't my role to soothe the other two any longer. All along I'd been the peacemaker, the soother, the one who made light of the never-ending danger we'd faced fighting the Hive. Gunnar was a moody fuck and quick to anger. Hell, Erik had always just been downright angry. Sad, even. I'd always kept my feelings in check to help tame those two. But now, with Sophia, I couldn't do that. I was just as raw and angry and frustrated as the others. I couldn't tame them any longer. I could barely tame myself when it came to Sophia and danger.

But she'd soothed me. Eased my worries, my fears. My anger. It was her job now to tend to all three of us and I relished that. I needed it. I needed to know I could be angry or upset, mad or even fucking pissed and she wouldn't care. She'd hug me, or wash my back, and make it all better again.

We belonged to her. And now, it was time for her to belong to all of us. Forever.

Gunnar held out his hand. "Come, love. Let's make you ours."

11

Ours. Oh, yes. I'd just fucked Gunnar—well, he'd actually fucked *me* and very thoroughly—just a short time ago. In the few hours since, everything changed. We'd found the guy who'd wanted me dead. Dorn had held an ion pistol to my head and I'd realized exactly how much my mates meant to me.

I'd been willing to die to protect Gunnar. No second guessing, no doubts. I'd fallen in love with my mates faster than should be possible. But that was, after all, exactly what Warden Egara at the bride processing center had promised me. The matching process was designed to find mates perfect for me. And, with that asshole's hand around my throat and gun to my head, I realized they were perfect.

Rolf charmed and beguiled me with his golden good looks and smart wit. Erik's passion and dedication, outspoken loyalty and dirty talk, combined with the fact that he looked like a Viking god, made me long to be in his arms. And Gunnar, my dark, brooding alpha male, had a heart so selfless, so dedicated to service and duty, that I ached each time I looked at him.

While I'd known I wanted all three of my Viken warriors before, the near-death experience only strengthened my resolve. These three brave, possessive, dominant guys were mine. They wanted me.

The way they were staring at me left no doubt. Gunnar's jaw was clenched tightly. Erik's eyes blazed with heat. Rolf's usually relaxed body seemed poised to pounce. And all three of them had cocks that could pound nails. Or fill me up, every which way.

Yes, please.

Just as I'd told Rolf, it had been a two-year nightmare. It all started with the phone call from the doctor's office, the visit where we learned of my mother's cancer. The medicine she'd need to live. The cost. The Corellis. The bargain. Everything I'd done for them had been worth it. Yes, I'd done bad things. Smuggled drugs and money into the country, but it had given my mother an extra six months.

I hadn't walked away from the Corellis when I walked away from my mother's grave. They'd kept their thumb on me, forcing me to continue. My job, my art, hell, the entire art world lost its color, its brilliance. They'd ruined my life. And when I'd been arrested for my crimes, they hadn't saved me. I'd been tossed into jail, sentenced to twenty-five years—twenty-five!—for the crime of loving my mother too much.

But every moment, every second of that torturous time had led me to this moment, to these Vikens. My mates. Fate? Perhaps. If I hadn't sought out the Corellis, made a deal with them, none of this would have happened. I wouldn't be on Viken.

This was where I belonged. There was nothing—or no one—on Earth for me. My mother would want me to follow my passions, just as she always had with my art. But now, my world showed brightly not from paints and swirls of color, but because of Gunnar, Rolf and Erik.

She would have loved them. Shocked perhaps that I had three husbands, but I didn't doubt their love for me. They hadn't said it aloud, for it had been too soon, but they showed it.

And now, with Gunnar's hand out, I could have it all. I could truly, completely belong to them. All I had to do was place my palm in his. The three of them would do the rest.

I didn't doubt, didn't question, didn't even think when I reached out for him. As soon as our hands met, he pulled me from the tub and into his arms, uncaring that I was dripping wet.

He kissed me, fierce and dark and carnal. All his pent-up passion, and anger, frustration, need—every emotion —poured from him and into the kiss.

I took it all, everything he had to give me.

A cloth rubbed over my back, drying my skin, not once did Gunnar lift his head.

Hands on my shoulders spun me about, tearing our

lips apart. A wicked grin on Erik's face was all I saw with my passion-filled eyes before his mouth took over. He tasted different, his need different. Hotter, sharper, his kiss consumed me. Where Gunnar was all dark passion, Erik was all heat, fire. Brilliance.

I felt Gunnar's hard chest against my back, Erik at my front. I was between them, no room to move, to do anything but feel. But something was missing. No, someone.

I turned my head, breathed out the name. "Rolf."

He was there beside me, smiling at me, stroking my wet hair. "Need me, too?"

I nodded. "I need all of you."

He kissed me then, his hands cupping my face as Erik's and Gunnar's hands ran over me, cupping my breasts, plucking my nipples, stroking over the curve of my bottom, slipping between my thighs to stroke my most sensitive flesh.

I whimpered at their onslaught to my senses. It was overwhelming.

Rolf's lips left mine and I was lifted into the air, carried from the side of the bathtub and into the bedroom, lowered to stand on my feet directly beside the bed.

"I may have taken you a few hours ago, love, but I need you again," Gunnar said.

Erik growled. "We haven't taken her tonight."

"Your cock should be resting," Rolf added, the corner of his mouth tipping up. "Erik and I can handle this if you're not up to it."

All of us glanced at Gunnar's cock. It was far from resting.

"You think any of our cocks will be rested for the next few days?"

My inner walls clenched at the idea of them taking me so frequently. My arousal dripped down my thighs.

"Days?" Erik added. "Weeks."

Rolf shook his head. "Months."

"Forever," I replied, trying to end this silly boy feud. "I will never be tired of you three. Ever."

They moved toward me as a group. Stepping back, I bumped into the bed, dropping onto it so I was seated directly before all three of them. All three of their big, hard, eager cocks bobbed directly in front of my face.

Lifting a finger, I lightly swiped the fluid seeping from all three of their tips. I glanced up at them through my lashes, knowing the power of this slick essence.

I felt the heat of it, the intensity of the fluid as it touched just my fingertip, but when I lifted it to my mouth, tasted their mixed flavor, I almost came. It was so powerful, this need I had for them, for it matched their need for me. This seed, the power of it, was made for me. Only me. I tasted their *power*, their *need*, their *love*.

I wanted it. I wanted them. I wanted everything.

I'd given up Earth and gained the universe.

––––––

Gunnar

She was so beautiful, so perfect before us. The impish look in her eyes was quickly replaced with such heated desire I was surprised she didn't burst into flames. When she'd licked our combined seed, her body responded and need washed over her. Her nipples tightened, her skin flushed, her eyes fell closed, her muscles softened. I knew her pussy was dripping; I could scent her musky arousal.

This wasn't the club. This was our bed where we would truly make Sophia ours.

Now.

"I took you hard earlier in the club. This time, it won't be fucking, love."

Rolf shook his head as he went and settled onto the bed, his head resting on the pillows. Quirking a finger, he beckoned Sophia toward him.

She looked at him, then to Erik, then me. Licked her lips. "No, not fucking," she repeated as she crawled naked so she was close enough to kiss him. Her breasts fell heavily beneath her and I couldn't help but stroke a hand over her lush ass. Erik went around the bed and knelt on the other side of her.

She was surrounded and soon, she would be filled. She would take all of us.

"Straddle me." Rolf's words were intermixed with kisses and she threw a leg over his waist, not breaking the kiss.

He kissed her for a long, slow minute, but I knew what Rolf wanted, what he always wanted.

Sophia squealed as he lifted her, moving her so that her pussy settled directly over his mouth. Erik and I watched as Rolf worked her with his mouth, her head thrown back and her hips grinding into his chin as Rolf pleasured her.

Unable to resist, Erik leaned forward and took her

breast in his mouth, tugging and suckling her as Rolf worked her wet pussy from below.

Our mate placed her hands on the thick headboard, bracing herself as Erik's hand drifted lower, to tease her back entrance. The virgin ass that would soon be filled with his cock.

I let them play, Sophia's pleased gasps and moans an aphrodisiac all their own. When Erik lifted his head from Sophia's breast with a nod to me, I tossed him the tube of thickened oil he would need to prepare our mate's ass for his cock.

She was ready to take all of us. She'd been ready since the club.

Grinning, Erik squeezed a large amount onto his fingers, coating them.

Patience at an end, I lay down next to Rolf and lifted Sophia from his body, settling her over mine.

"Gunnar!" Sophia squealed like a little girl and I actually chuckled as I settled her hips low, my hard cock pressed between us. "I'm going to fuck you, mate."

"God, hurry up!" Sophia demanded as Erik and Rolf both chuckled.

In the future, I'd spank her ass for such an outburst, make her wait. Make her beg. But right now, I couldn't think past the need to be inside her hot, wet pussy. I needed to claim her, mark her, make sure she belonged to us without question.

I lifted her and tilted my hips, sliding her hot core down over my hard cock in one long, smooth glide.

Sophia groaned and leaned forward, claiming my lips in a kiss that stole my heart and my breath. She claimed me with her kiss, marked my heart and soul as her own. I buried my hands in her hair and held her to me, devoured her love like a man dying of hunger as I thrust up once. Twice. Hard. Driving deeper.

Beside me, Rolf chuckled. "Share, Gunnar. That mouth is mine."

The sound of a sharp slap filled the room and Sophia jerked on top of me as Erik spanked her ass. The motion made me moan and I broke the kiss.

"Fine, hurry the fuck up. I can't hold out for long."

"Move, Gunnar. Shift to the side." Rolf was on his knees near my shoulder, his hard cock standing at attention and level with Sophia's head. I lifted her a bit, angling her upper torso toward Rolf as Erik knelt below us, his hands on Sophia's ass.

"No, move this way. I need your legs over the edge," Erik insisted.

Sophia laughed and I smiled up into her eager gaze as I moved us both until her knees were on the edge of the bed, my much longer legs bent at the knee to hang over the side, my feet on the floor. My cock in her pussy, where it belonged.

Erik stood behind her, kneading her ass, playing with her sensitive bottom. He took his time, making sure Sophia was ready for him there, coating her insides with the slick oil. Rolf had moved with us, kneeling once more at my shoulder. All Sophia need do to take him into her mouth was lean her shoulders to the side and wrap those luscious lips around his cock.

Buried deep inside Sophia's tight pussy, I felt Erik's two fingers slide inside her body. He filled her with them, moving in and out as her pussy clenched down on my cock like a clamp and I groaned at Erik's prolonged teasing.

"By the gods, Erik. Fuck her. Now."

Wrapping my hand about her waist, I pulled Sophia toward me, locked her abdomen to mine so her ass tilted up toward Erik like an offering. With Rolf's hand cupping her nape and my hands on her sides, she wasn't pinned, but she would know we held her. That we had her exactly where we wanted her.

Erik teased us all, sliding his slick fingers over her back entrance. Her muscles tightened and quivered as he began to circle a finger, then press inward, deeper this time.

She gasped and Rolf bent low, claiming her mouth as she wiggled her hips a bit. I glanced quickly to Erik, who nodded and proceeded to stretch her open enough to slip three fingers inside. Her pussy stretched as he filled her, tight as a fist around my cock.

"Oh, God." Sophia tore her lips from Rolf's kiss and a soft moan escaped her lips. Erik grinned with triumph, taking her response as an invitation to continue.

"Soon, love, we'll all be inside you," Erik promised. His fingers moved inside her, going deeper and deeper, then pulling back, mimicking what his cock would do in short order.

Rolf released her neck and pulled back. Their eyes met and held. While Erik was the one setting her nerves aflame deep in her virgin ass, Rolf had her sole attention. "Take my cock, Sophia. Suck it deep," he murmured. His usual congenial tone was rough with need.

Erik slipped his fingers from her as she aligned her mouth over Rolf's cock. I knew the second his pre-cum touched her lips, for her head fell back and she moaned. Sinking down on me, she took Rolf deep in her mouth, moving forward until he disappeared completely and I saw the bulge of his cock at the top of her throat.

"Yes," Rolf could barely breathe as she fucked him with her beautiful mouth.

I slid my hands from her waist to her breasts, sliding my fingers between our bodies to play with her hard nipples. She groaned and wiggled, pulled back her head until only the tip of Rolf's cock was in her mouth, then taking him deep once more.

I held still, but not for long. No Viken warrior could survive a pussy like Sophia's without moving.

Erik added more lube to his fingers and continued his preparation, taking his sweet time, enjoying the anal play. I could do nothing but wait, but I was enjoying the view. Enjoying seeing our mate between us, getting all our attentions. Loving it. Loving us.

I hadn't spoken the words, but there was no doubt. She had our hearts as much as we had hers.

Erik nodded to me, breaking me from my romantic notions.

"She's ready. That's right, love," Erik said, coating his cock liberally with the lube. "I'm going to fuck you now."

She nodded, her dark hair sliding over her shoulders as Rolf popped free from her mouth. "Yes," she whispered. "Do it."

"Do you accept us as your mates, Sophia? Because this is forever," I said.

Her eyes met mine, and though they were glazed with

passion, I saw a strange curiosity there. "Is this the claiming ceremony?"

"Yes," Rolf told her, touching her cheek. "There's no going back, love. We'll be yours forever."

"Yes," she repeated. "I want you. All three of you." Her hips jerked over my cock and I gritted my teeth as I felt the large bulk of Erik's cock slide inside her body.

"That's my cock, relax," Erik instructed. "Deep breath. Good, let it out. Yes, like that. Once more. Good, yes, I'm in."

Sophia groaned, her eyes falling closed, allowing her a moment to savor the feel of two cocks. I knew Erik's precum seeped into her, easing the claiming. She wanted it, but the additional seed power would make it even better for her.

She was ours, completely. The claiming had begun. There was no going back.

She was ours.

Our mate.

Our future.

———

SOPHIA

ERIK PRESSED FORWARD, SPREADING ME OPEN WITH HIS huge cock. The sharp sting faded to an agony of sensation. I'd never been so full. So fucked.

Gunnar's cock was balls deep in my wet pussy, so large and demanding that I'd nearly had an orgasm just from the feel of him stretching me open.

With both of my mates buried deep, I looked up into Rolf's eyes, golden Rolf, and smiled. The taste of his precum lingered on my tongue, the burning heat of it down my throat proof that I was not immune to his seed power, to the chemical cocktail in his seed that made me a horny, crazy mess. "You want in on this action?"

He looked confused by my Earth slang, but took me literally. "Yes, mate. I want to fuck that pretty little mouth."

I imagined some unsuspecting woman walking into a bride processing center on Earth and reliving *this*. Gunnar beneath me, playing with my breasts as his cock filled me from below. Erik behind me, his cock in my ass, making me burn, and writhe, and feel pinned. Helpless. Conquered in the most elemental way imaginable. And Rolf looking down on me with so much longing, such lust, that I could no more deny him than cut my own heart from my chest.

These men were mine. Mine. Forever. And I'd give them anything they wanted. Anything they needed.

With a grin, I circled the tip of Rolf's cock with my tongue and watched him tremble as I teased him.

Smack!

Smack!

Smack!

"Don't tease him, mate. Suck his cock." Erik's palm landed on my ass with a sharp crack and I cried out, jerking forward to escape him. But Gunnar's hands had returned to my hips, and he held me in place as Erik spanked me, his cock buried deep, right next to Gunnar's. I'd never been so full. So stretched.

The added sensation of the stinging on my bottom

was too much, and I tried to escape, but Gunnar held me in place as Rolf shook his head, dangling his cock in front of my face, rubbing pre-cum on my lips. "Do you want us to stop?" He leaned over as I licked my lips clean, enjoyed the burn of his essence on my tongue. He pressed his lips to my ear. "Or do you want us to come inside you, fuck you raw until you lose control, until you scream?"

He knelt before me and all three of my men stopped moving, waiting for me to answer. Stop now? Or let them fill me, take me. Claim me. Fuck me until I lost my mind.

"Come closer." I issued the order to Rolf as I pushed back onto Erik's cock and squeezed my inner muscles to torment Gunnar, and his iron control, beneath me. When Rolf's cock was where I wanted it, I looked over my shoulder at Erik. "I love you, Erik. I want you to fuck me. Don't stop. Don't ever stop."

Smack!

Erik struck my ass and I groaned as the heat spread. "Damn it, female. That's for telling me now, when I can't kiss you."

I grinned at him, unrepentant as he replied, "I love you, Sophia. You're mine."

I turned my attention to Gunnar, planting a soft, lingering kiss on his lips so he would know he was mine, too. They were all mine. Lifting my head, I stared into his eyes. "I love you."

He pulled me back down for a merciless clash of tongue and teeth, his kiss so carnal and full of need that my pussy pulsed around him in response. "I love you, mate."

Rolf waited patiently as I turned to him. Just for fun, I licked his cock again, swirling my tongue around the tip like I would a melting ice-cream cone. He grinned at me. "You're going to be trouble, mate. I can just tell."

I smiled. "I love you, too, Rolf."

"I love you, Sophia."

Just like that, we were a family. I knew they would never leave me and I would never tire of their attentions.

Shifting my hips forward, I pulled away from both Gunnar's and Erik's cocks. When they both moved toward me in protest, I slammed back down on them, hard. Deep. They both groaned and I took advantage of the moment, sucking Rolf's cock until it hit the back of my throat.

Tension built in the air. Snapped. Rolf grabbed my hair and pulled out of my mouth, pushing deep over and over. I don't know if they were coordinating purposely or not, but Erik's rhythm matched Rolf's as one took my mouth and the other my ass. In together. Out together. In. Out.

Shaking with pent-up lust, I tilted my hips, shifting forward and back, trying to rub my clit against Gunnar's rock-hard body. Beneath me, he moaned, his massive chest glistening with heat and sweat as I rode him and Erik's cock rubbed us both deep inside me.

When Gunnar's large hand slid between our bodies to rub my clit, my shout of encouragement was garbled by Rolf's huge cock in my mouth. But Gunnar heard me, his fingers sliding under me, exactly where I wanted him.

"Ride me, Sophia. Give me your clit. Fuck my fingers, too."

My eyes rolled back into my head as Erik shifted balls deep in my ass. Gunnar thrust up from the bed, driving up into me with his cock and shoving my clit onto his fingers. Rolf thrust deep, pulled back. Thrust.

The orgasm rolled through me and my legs jerked as I clamped down on Erik's cock in my ass and Gunnar's cock in my core. Erik's cock I sucked deep, holding him until I was dizzy from lack of oxygen.

My release spurred them on and they all moved, thrusting and withdrawing in wild abandon. Their course and uncontrolled rhythms drove me wild, pushing me toward another orgasm.

Rolf lost it first. He came down my throat, his seed power like an inferno of need spreading through me. My pussy clamped down on Gunnar as I came again. My release caused Erik and Gunnar to lose control, their cocks spilling inside me as they both pressed deep and held, as if trying to fill me up with their seed as well.

The extra dose of Viken seed power made me come again, my whole body felt like it had been dipped in a hot bath. My blood was on fire, the orgasm forced every muscle in my body to clench and release as my pussy went into its final spasm.

When it was over, I collapsed against Gunnar's chest, my own body heaving for breath. Rolf rolled onto his side beside me, his hand stroking through my hair and over my back with slow, gentle strokes. Erik pulled his cock from me slowly, as if reluctant to leave, and lay down on Gunnar's other side. I turned to face him and tried to smile, but I felt too damn good, even for that.

Erik's eyes were dark and serious as he reached over and tucked a stray piece of hair behind my ear. His fingers shook. "We're never letting you go."

"Never," Rolf agreed.

Gunnar's response, with his cock still inside me, was to lift his hips and make me gasp in aftershock as his body rubbed my sensitive clit. "Forever, Sophia."

I laid my head down over Gunnar's beating heart and closed my eyes, listened to the strong, steady beat. "Forever," I agreed.

EPILOGUE

*S*ophia, *Viken United, Princess Allayna's 1st Birthday Party*

SOFT MUSIC PLAYED IN THE BACKGROUND, SOMETHING I'D expect from a string quartet back home, but with a strange ringing notes like harp music. Warm lighting flickered on the walls from strange lanterns decorated with the sword, shield and spear designs of the three sectors, the silhouettes creating strange and unusual shadows that shifted and moved all around me. The huge ballroom was filled as the people of Viken United laughed and danced. The women were dressed to excess, their dresses long, elegant and brightly colored. Their elaborate hair designs, all adorned with flowers, jewels or sparkles of some variety, turned the dance floor into a glittering flow of beauty.

And I was here. My gown was a deep, vibrant orange, the color of a fall sunset, and fell to my feet. Heavy around my neck were the sparkling cut jewels that draped my chest and wrists like lightning trapped inside amber. I'd never seen anything like it before. The gems, a gift from Erik, had belonged to his mother. He'd claimed, as he'd draped them around my neck, that he'd never thought to see them on another woman.

He honored me, and I knew my mate. Knew what he'd gone through to let go of the pain of his past. Giving me the necklace was proof that he'd let go of the past, but yet have his mother live on. Seeing me wear what belonged to her kept her alive for him, even though she was long, long gone. He'd lost a family when his parents died, but he'd gained a new one. One with a future so bright it made my eyes tear.

We were all three ready to move on now, to focus on what would come next.

Rolf and Erik had run off on some secret business, but Gunnar stood beside me and I smiled up at him. He looked spectacular in his usual black, but the contentment I saw in his eyes when he looked down at me was my true joy.

"You are so beautiful all I can think about is fucking you."

I burst out laughing. Oh, yes. That was my Gunnar. Blunt. Crude. So damn hot and demanding. I'd let him do whatever he wanted to me, to my body, and he knew it. "Behave, Gunnar. It took the stylist over an hour to do my hair," I teased him, but slid my hand into his, craving his touch.

That small contact must have been enough, for he grunted and led me onto the dance floor. I didn't know the steps, but he pulled me close and simply carried me around like a small girl as he followed the steps of the Viken dance. I felt his love, felt it differently than when I first arrived. Before, it had been a powerful protectiveness, yet it felt distant. Now, I knew he gave me everything. All of him.

"I didn't know you knew how to dance."

"I'm a simple man with simple needs."

I tried to make sense of that one. "And dancing is a need?"

Gunnar grinned and lowered his lips so they caressed my ear as he replied, "No, love. Holding a beautiful woman is the need. Dancing is what I will suffer to hold you."

Ah, so, not so different from Earth men after all.

I smiled and relaxed into his embrace as the music swelled around us. I paid no attention to where he led me, content to be in his arms until the music stopped.

As the crowd parted, Gunnar set me on my feet before him and settled his hands on my shoulders. The stance was a blatant claiming, and I welcomed it. I was proud to be his. And I wanted every woman in the room to know he was mine. So very mine.

And speaking of mine, where were my other mates? "Where are Erik and Rolf? They've been gone a long time."

"Ten minutes is not a long time."

I sighed. "It feels like longer." I leaned against my mate, pressing my back to his chest and he held me, as I'd known he would, while the caterers, or cooks, or whatever the hell they called them on this planet rolled out a huge, pink-and-white birthday cake. The cake was as fancy and elaborate as any wedding cake I'd ever seen back home, with multiple layers, tiered dividers separating the entire confection into about twenty different sections.

At the front was a small, round cake with bright pink flowers and one candle, for the birthday girl.

"Setting fire to a candle and blowing it out is an odd birthing day tradition."

I smiled then, knowing Leah was the reason behind the solitary candle. "You don't just blow out the candle. You blow it out and make a wish."

"And what do you wish for, my mate?"

I had to think about that one for a minute. "I don't know. I have everything I ever wanted."

Gunnar's hold tightened in response as Leah and her three mates stepped out from behind a doorway that must lead to the royal quarters.

The little princess was dressed in a fluffy pink dress. She had ribbons in her red hair and her cheeks were rosy to match her outfit. Her big blue eyes were glassy, as if she'd just woken from a long nap. She sat in her mother's arms content and smiled at every new face as the Queen walked past.

Little Princess Allayna was absolutely adorable. It was no wonder the people of Viken had united behind her claim to the throne.

Her pudgy little baby hand reached up to one of her fathers, I couldn't tell them apart yet, and he smiled at her but did not lift her from her mother's arms.

Leah looked small surrounded by her men. But she practically glowed with happiness and I knew every single one of her mates would die for her, kill for her, was completely and irrevocably committed to her.

Just like mine were to me.

Somehow, I'd gone from a shit life on Earth to the most amazing, fulfilling life I could have dreamed.

I wrapped my arms around my stomach as I watched Leah wait for one of the Kings to light that little birthday candle. The Vikens around us broke out in their version of a birthday song and when it was over, Leah looked at me and nodded as she began singing the familiar *Happy Birthday* tune. Delighted to be part of merging old traditions with new, I sang along with her and cheered when Leah bent low and *helped* her little princess blow out the solitary candle.

Cheers broke out and little Allayna clapped her hands and reached for her daddy. She didn't care about birthday cake or presents. I doubted she'd even understand how to use the pencils and paper I got for her to start her off as a budding artist. She just wanted to be loved. Cuddled. Protected.

Held.

I wanted soft skin and baby giggles. I wanted to be a mother, so damn much. I wanted to watch a little one scramble and crawl all over a stoic Gunnar, laugh at Rolf's teasing, and tug on Erik's long hair, forcing him to play.

Tears gathered in my eyes as I watched the happy family and my hands drifted low, over my abdomen, where I hoped to one day create a special, precious someone. Like Leah, it would not matter to me which of my mates was the biological father, for I loved them all.

Gunnar noticed the position of my hands, of course, and his large ones shifted to wrap around me and cover mine, holding them in place when I would have dropped or moved them away. He always noticed everything I did, every move I made, every expression. Sometimes, I wondered if he could somehow sense my very heart beating.

His breath was hot in my ear as he bent over me. "Do you want a child, Sophia?"

I couldn't lie. There was no reason to. "Yes."

Gunnar's hands tightened convulsively over mine and a faint tremble passed through him where he pressed to my back. I turned around and wrapped my arms around him as the celebration resumed. The cake was cut, the sugary treat new to the people gathered. Judging from the delighted sounds of surprise around the room, Leah had just corrupted an entire planet.

I wanted a piece of that cake. Badly. But I really wanted to know where the hell my other two mates were.

When Gunnar tried to lead me back onto the dance floor, I pulled back. "No, Gunnar. Where are Rolf and Erik?"

"They will return soon."

"So you said, but where did they go?" My patience was wearing thin. I was starting to feel like they were keeping something from me, something bad.

Had the VSS made a new threat? Was one of them injured?

My heart raced and I tugged free of Gunnar's hold. Turning on my heel, I took three steps before Gunnar's hand wrapped around my waist, and the Queen's voice carried over some kind of speaker system.

"Sophia Antonelli of Earth. Please come forward and present yourself to the Queen of Viken."

Holy fucking shit.

I froze. Gunnar chuckled, so I hit him in the chest. "You knew about this? What is going on?"

He raised a brow and walked me toward the sound of the Queen's voice. She'd moved sometime during the cake cutting and the dancing and I could just make out her head above the crowd on some sort of stage.

In no time at all I stood before her and had no freaking clue what I was supposed to do. Bow? Curtsy—whatever the hell that was? Kneel? I'd never been formally presented to royalty before.

I settled for a slight dip of my knees and what I hoped didn't look ridiculous, but Leah just laughed and motioned for me to come up onstage and stand beside her.

When I was up on the raised platform, I looked out over a crowd of hundreds of Viken citizens, all silent, waiting for their queen's next words. I met Gunnar's eyes, and the warmth and pride I saw there helped me relax enough to get air in and out of my lungs. I didn't like being the center of so much attention. Ever.

Leah locked her arm with mine and continued to speak. "My friends, this is Sophia Antonelli, mate to Gunnar, Erik and Rolf of Viken United. She came to us, like I did, as an Interstellar Bride from Earth."

Polite applause broke out, but lasted just a few seconds before silence settled once more. Leah took a deep breath.

"Not long ago, those who wish to destroy the new peace we enjoy on Viken made an attempt on my daughter's life."

Gasps and outrage filled the room, angry shouts mixed with shocked denials as Leah continued.

"But this woman, this stranger, saved Princess Allayna's life. She saved my life. And then, she bravely traveled to Central City and helped our royal guards track down the man responsible for the attack."

Shocked silence at that. I gave a halfhearted shrug. "The Queen of a planet calls and asks for a favor, well? What were we going to say?

Leah pulled back and looked at me with tears in her eyes. "Actually, I made a trade."

"Trade?"

Leah nodded. "Yep. They all wanted to be the first to have authentic alien art in their museums. The Smithsonian and The Louvre made me the best offers."

"I don't know what to say." Thank you seemed grossly inadequate.

"You saved Allayna. I could never, ever repay you. There isn't enough art in the universe to repay you."

I wiped at the tears slipping down my own cheeks. "I didn't do anything. Just got sent to the wrong place at the right time."

Leah shook her head. "No. You fought. You took our place, willing or not. You helped track down a traitor. You were brave and wild and tough, everything I'd expect from a New Yorker."

I smiled and hugged her one more time, ready to inspect the treasure trove behind me as one of the Kings brought little Allayna forward. When Leah stepped back, I expected the King to hand his precious princess to her mother. Instead, he placed the adorable cherub in my arms.

The party guests roared their approval as my mates came forward, surrounding me with their love.

Leah whooped and hollered like only a wild city girl could for a few seconds, before turning to me with a sparkle in her eye I'd not noticed before. She reached for her daughter and Allayna held out her arms, eager to be with her favorite person in the world.

I missed her small body immediately, but Leah's knowing grin stopped me cold.

"What?"

"Being Queen has perks."

"So you said." I raised my brow. "Leah?"

Leah's eyes filled with joy as she looked at her daughter, then back at me, deliberately dropping her gaze to my stomach, holding it there for a full three seconds before looking me in the eye.

My hands flew to my abdomen and I tried not to hope. "Leah, what perks?"

"I know everything that goes on in this place. And I know you went to medical after your adventure in Central City."

"And?"

"Viken medicine is a lot more advanced than ours."

"And?" I was ready to pounce on her if she didn't start talking.

"Twins." Her smile was radiant as she looked at each of my mates in turn. "And they'll be born just in time to keep Allayna's little sister company. Maybe they'll have tea parties. Hell, art parties. And we can have so much fun dressing them up. Ribbons and dresses and I'm going to ask my guys to import some *Disney* movies. You know, like *Cinderella* and *Beauty and the Beast.*"

"*Frozen* and *Tangled.*" I had to get my requests in now. "And you said—you're pregnant?"

"Yes! We both are!" Leah squealed. "Oh, my God, Sophia! I can't wait. It'll be so much more fun with you here."

"Twin girls?" Erik materialized at my side and looked over my shoulder at the Queen.

"That's what the doctor told me," Leah said.

Erik whooped and swung me around in a circle, spinning me until I was dizzy and the long tail of his hair swung behind his neck like a rope, smacking Rolf's grinning face on the cheek.

Rolf stopped him and the moment my feet hit the ground, Rolf, my golden warrior, kissed me like I was delicate china.

And Gunnar, my big, strong, bossy brute wiped tears from his dark eyes as all three of my men surrounded me.

I was lucky. So damn lucky. And loved, more than I could have ever imagined.

And I was wearing orange.

Go figure.

A SPECIAL THANK YOU TO MY READERS...

Want more? I've got *hidden* bonus content on my web site *exclusively* for those on my <u>mailing list.</u>

If you are already on my email list, you don't need to do a thing! Simply scroll to the bottom of my newsletter emails and click on the *super-secret* link.

Not a member? What are you waiting for? In addition to ALL of my bonus content (great new stuff will be added regularly) you will be the first to hear about my newest release the second it hits the stores—AND you will get a free book as a special welcome gift.

Sign up now! http://freescifiromance.com

FIND YOUR INTERSTELLAR MATCH!

YOUR mate is out there. Take the test today and discover your perfect match. Are you ready for a sexy alien mate (or two)?

VOLUNTEER NOW!

interstellarbridesprogram.com

DO YOU LOVE AUDIOBOOKS?

Grace Goodwin's books are now available as audiobooks...everywhere.

LET'S TALK SPOILER ROOM!

Interested in joining my **Sci-Fi Squad**? Meet new like-minded sci-fi romance fanatics and chat with Grace! Get excerpts, cover reveals and sneak peeks before anyone else. Be part of a private Facebook group that shares pictures and fun news! Join here:

https://www.facebook.com/groups/scifisquad/

***

Want to talk about Grace Goodwin books with others? Join the **SPOILER ROOM** and spoil away! Your GG BFFs are waiting! (And so is Grace)

Join here:

https://www.facebook.com/groups/ggspoilerroom/

GET A FREE BOOK!

JOIN MY MAILING LIST TO BE THE FIRST TO KNOW OF NEW RELEASES, FREE BOOKS, SPECIAL PRICES AND OTHER AUTHOR GIVEAWAYS.

http://freescifiromance.com

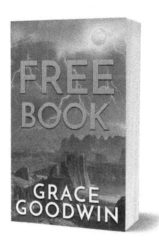

ALSO BY GRACE GOODWIN

Surrender to the Cyborgs

Mated to the Cyborgs

Cyborg Seduction

Her Cyborg Beast

Cyborg Fever

Rogue Cyborg

Cyborg's Secret Baby

Her Cyborg Warriors

Interstellar Brides® Program: The Virgins

The Alien's Mate

Claiming His Virgin

His Virgin Mate

His Virgin Bride

Interstellar Brides® Program: Ascension Saga

Ascension Saga, book 1

Ascension Saga, book 2

Ascension Saga, book 3

Trinity: Ascension Saga - Volume 1

Ascension Saga, book 4

Ascension Saga, book 5

Ascension Saga, book 6

Faith: Ascension Saga - Volume 2

Ascension Saga, book 7

Ascension Saga, book 8

Ascension Saga, book 9

Destiny: Ascension Saga - Volume 3

Other Books

Their Conquered Bride

Wild Wolf Claiming: A Howl's Romance

ABOUT GRACE

Grace Goodwin is a USA Today and international bestselling author of Sci-Fi and Paranormal romance with more than one million books sold. Grace's titles are available worldwide in multiple languages in ebook, print and audio formats. Two best friends, one left-brained, the other right-brained, make up the award-winning writing duo that is Grace Goodwin.

They are both mothers, escape room enthusiasts, avid readers and intrepid defenders of their preferred beverages. (There may or may not be an ongoing tea vs. coffee war occurring during their daily communications.) Grace loves to hear from readers!

All of Grace's books can be read as sexy, stand-alone adventures. But be careful, she likes her heroes hot and her love scenes hotter. You have been warned...

www.gracegoodwin.com
gracegoodwinauthor@gmail.com